DON'T WASTE YOUR PAIN

W. C. Wilson

Copyright © 2022 by W. C. Wilson

ISBN | 978-0-578-99426-0

All rights reserved.

Table of Contents

Preface 1
Introduction 5

Section I
IDOLIZING YOUR PAST

Chapter 1: Your Past was Never Meant to Become an Idol 9
Chapter 2: The Idol of Missed Opportunities: Never Abandon God 29
Chapter 3: God is Not the Enemy 39
Chapter 4: The Envy that is Birthed 47
Chapter 5: Problems Associated with Old Habits 54
Chapter 6: Developing New Habits 76

Section II
Allowing Pain to Fuel You

Chapter 7: Fueled by Pain 101
Chapter 8: Avoid the Pain 105
Chapter 9: Retool and Live 116

Section III
Pain: Don't Waste It

Chapter 10: Don't Waste Your Pain 129
Chapter 11: Conclusion 135

ACKNOWLEDGEMENT

First giving all honor to my Heavenly Father, the LORD Jesus Christ, and the Holy Spirit. I am only here by the grace of God, I am only saved by the blood of the Lamb, and I am led by the Holy Spirit.

To my family, my inspiring wife Janine the writer in the family; thank you for encouraging me and believing in me through this long process. To my supportive children, Ania, Nadia and Cyrus; thank you for listening to excerpts and telling me to keep writing. They are the reason why I keep dreaming and believing and going.

To my deceased parents, W. C. Wilson Sr., and Margaret Wilson, who also inspired me to always work hard and to finish strong. And to my siblings, Monica, Veronica, Danita and Connie, my forever cheering section.

And finally, to my beloved, maternal grandmother, who taught me so much about life, through her own victories and struggles, Carrie James, rest on Big Momma.

DON'T WASTE YOUR PAIN

Preface

"In this life you will have trouble", (John 16:33 ESV).
"Count it all joy, my brothers, when you meet trials of various kinds", (James 1:2 ESV).

These are two often-recited Bible verses that offer words of encouragement when read in context of the associated scripture. However, if you are like me you prefer to turn to the Bible for words that suggest "blessings, come to me now," and "I have a feeling everything is going to be alright.".

Instead, from the aforementioned verses a person can discern that life is invariably filled with trouble, trials, and some unwanted, unwelcome adversity; prompting a sure realization we will all experience our fair share in our lifetime. Unfortunately, if we focus too heavily on moments like these, we can easily overlook one important fact: goodness is often birthed through troubles, trials, and sometimes, adversities.

This book was penned for the sole purpose of highlighting one important truth: you can become so paralyzed by the painful experiences of your past, you succumb to living the rest of your life stuck in the quicksand of despair. You refuse to struggle to break free because you have already decided to give up. I hope to motivate you to use your pain to generate positive movement as you fight to become an overcomer and not an underachiever. Allow me to illustrate.

Most mothers describe the process of childbirth as difficult, painful, and laborious. When an expecting mother has given her all during childbirth and her baby has not fully descended the birth canal, she chooses to keep pushing with all her strength. She makes the conscientious choice to push through those painful contractions because she knows a life depends on her being persistent, even in her pain. Contractions cause the mother pain, but they also assist the movement of the baby down the birth canal. It is the mother's endurance during those painful moments of childbirth that allow her to rejoice once she has finally given birth because she was willing to push through. Although it was indeed unbearable at times, she can look back over her ordeal and realize the experience was well worth the pain. No contractions, no labor; no labor, no childbirth.

A pearl is a sight to behold, but the oyster that produces the pearl must suffer before we can see such a beautiful jewel. A pearl is created inside an oyster only after foreign particles (grains of sand) become trapped inside the oyster's shell. The trapped particles cause tremendous irritation for the oyster, since it is unable to stop the cause or propel the particle outside the shell. All the while the irritation is occurring, something remarkable happens inside the oyster shell. Instead of succumbing to the irritation, the oyster uses its defense mechanism to coat the foreign particle until over time, a magnificent pearl is formed. Thus, a beautiful pearl is created because of the suffering and extreme irritation the oyster was forced to endure. No sand, no irritation; no irritation, no pearl. I am sure those who enjoy wearing pearls are glad that oysters have found a way to cope with uncontrollable irritation.

These are simply two examples that clearly illustrate how pain can foster change when the experience is not wasted.

Have you ever wondered why some people cite phenomenal success stories after explaining the tale of their adversity, while others only recount their adverse experiences? One reason is the first group kept moving forward during their struggle, using the challenge to fuel their determination rather than allowing it to cripple their motivation. Eventually, they benefited greatly because of the hurdles they faced and overcame along life's difficult journey, whereas the latter group decided the pain was too much to endure, and eventually gave in and gave up. Let this serve as a wakeup call to suggest that even when we inevitably meet up with adversity along life's highways, goodness can still prevail if we are willing to keep moving after breakdowns or even meltdowns.

As survivors who rise after each setback, we rejoice knowing that suffering tests and proves endurance, whereby endurance builds character, and character produces hope.

The adversities of life often lead to emotional and spiritual stamina, developing strength of character, and instilling hope for the hopeless moments we are bound to face. Focus on this: #YOUARESTILLHERE.

In summary, pain can force a pivot in direction and energy, propel you forward, help you achieve the unachievable, if you refuse to lose hope and never give up the fight.

Introduction

Throughout my lifetime, I have witnessed individuals trying to live with haunting regrets, painful memories they try to leave behind with little or no success. As a child, I saw close family members struggle with relationships due to their inability to recognize that "hurting people, hurt other people" and "victims eventually victimize others". Their lingering bitterness from unresolved emotional trauma evidently affected them more than perhaps they ever realized. As a result, they would often engage in unprovoked coarse discourse with other family members and close friends, creating lasting conflict and a trail of wounded, innocent victims running for cover following tense encounters. This dysfunctional behavior often perpetuated an avalanche of distress for those woven into their inner circle, with no hope of change, healing, or mending of hurt feelings.

As I grew older and heard many stories from those still struggling with painful memories, I sympathized and tried (unsuccessfully) to move them beyond the overwhelming sorrows caused by negative experiences they were unable to resolve. Unfortunately, misdeeds, mistakes, and sad memories can significantly hinder any ability and desire to heal. Furthermore, as they struggled to move forward, they were unable to live without their pain encumbering relationships and diminishing their aspiration and motivation to win. They hit the proverbial wall; unable to go over, around, or break through to discover inner peace.

When the past became a stumbling block, a stronghold causing emotional, psychological, and spiritual bondage, they struggled, consciously and unconsciously, unable to break free. As a result, they continue to drag around emotional baggage wherever they go. Their hearts, minds, and souls remain weighed down. My friends, no one should live constantly rehearsing the "un-editable" script of the past, allowing yesterday to wreak havoc on emotional well-being and spiritual development. This is easily a trap without a door or escape hatch.

If you find yourself in this place, allow me to breathe a few words of hope to ease your misery. No matter how deep our wounds are, or how much pain we have suffered, there is still hope for us all. If we are still breathing, there is hope for us to break free from past mistakes and regrets to live fruitful, prosperous lives despite our ominous past. Regardless of previous experiences, we can hope to live meaningful lives without wasting precious time wishing we made different or better choices, or wishing our lives had turned out differently. We are still alive and blessed with the opportunity of each new day.

We cannot change the past. However, we can learn to live in the moment rather than viewing life through rearview mirrors that often hide new scenes and potential opportunities. Pay careful attention to what I am saying. If you do not receive anything else, receive this: life is meant for us to live forward, not from an over-the-shoulder viewpoint. You cannot see the way forward clearly if you are constantly looking at regrets behind you. Refusing to live forward inevitably causes blind spots, hindering our ability to freely accept our own divinely orchestrated steps.

I hope by now I have your attention. If so, walk forward with me as we learn to experience freedom from our past so we can live freely in the present and future.

Section I

IDOLIZING YOUR PAST

Have you ever wondered why you cannot break free from some of the most disappointing moments or relationships in your life? The truth is, you yourself are the primary obstacle to finding the freedom you so desperately desire.

Chapter 1

Your Past was Never Meant to Become an Idol

Some of us have spent countless days and years wallowing in self-pity because of some painful experience that we failed to resolve and overcome. We never managed to forgive others, release ourselves, or make peace with our memories. Nor have we allowed ourselves the freedom to make mistakes as we travel along this difficult journey called life. Unfortunately, and unconsciously, pain carried over from unmelodious experiences can determine the color scheme we select that paints our perspective and perceptions of life. This less-than-vibrant color scheme tends to darken every waking moment, becoming another manifestation of our painful past.

Ironically, the constant attention we devote to distant experiences only serves to become an emotional idol—something worthless, useless, purposeless—that eventually produces stumbling blocks for our future. Dwelling on the past and paying homage to painful baggage becomes an unhealthy obsession that fosters idol worship if we fail to see the prevailing presence of God from every proverbial valley we walk through. First, let me state this: our past is just that. Yesterday has passed, the day before has passed, and all the days prior are long gone. Whether you accept and admit this or not, all of your yesterdays have packed up and moved on. That time is gone!

One of our biggest human faults is that we keep memories of pain on life support, never allowing emotional trauma to fade until left behind. The important details of our life stories are not that we went through some tough times. On the contrary, the moments that define us are when we go through tough times and find we are still here. The best way to preclude our past from negatively invading our present and future is to prevent the past from becoming an idol we unknowingly worship. How is it possible to prevent this if we are not aware of the disturbing habit in the first place? We must release and forget what lies behind us.

I realize this is easier said than done. If placing our past in a trunk and storing it away in the attic were easy, we all would have freed ourselves years ago. Work with me, if you will, because execution of this principle is as simple as the premise. If you are a Bible reader, there is a scripture in this for you. If you are not, take note: forgetting the past is a Biblical concept, not a Freudian ideology that allows us to prevail beyond our darkest memories.

The Apostle Paul wrote in an encouraging letter to the church at Philippi these emancipating words:

"Brothers and sisters, I do not consider myself yet to have taken hold of it. But one thing I do; forgetting what is behind and straining toward what is ahead, I press on to win the prize for which God has called me heavenward in Christ Jesus."

(Philippians 3:13-14 ESV)

I recognize this passage of scripture may not ring familiar to all of you right now. Some of you might not believe in the authority of the Bible over your lives. If not, you will have a great opportunity to see why scripture is so beneficial and important to everyday living. Locked away in the words of this text is your simple, yet profound solution to becoming permanently freed from your painful past.

Let me ask you this: If you had to determine Paul's purpose for delivering this instructional message to the church at Philippi, what would you conclude? Would you say Paul's purpose was singular in nature? Or would you conclude after examining his words that he had a multifaceted plan? Well, if you decided singular, then what would you conclude was his main purpose? Was it to help them to forget, successfully forge ahead, or simply to focus on being a prize winner in the Kingdom? If you settled on winning the prize, then I agree with you.

The other statements serve as the springboard Paul used to propel himself forward, detaching himself from his current state and moving beyond the restrictive corridors of his own mind. He had to move beyond the very thoughts that could derail him from winning the prize for which he was called. Paul refused to allow his thoughts to consume his every waking moment. He understood "memory is more than what we can consciously recall about events from the past."[1] Paul must have discerned "...that memory is the way past events affect future function."[2] Therefore, Paul refused to allow the memories of his past to become a drug that he pursued for a fix, serving to hinder his service to the LORD. Since Paul successfully achieved freedom for his journey, he desired the church to know this same freedom as well. Paul realized something only a few of us come to understand—that trying to live with a guilty conscience can gravely hinder freedom, wellness, and success.

Instead of succumbing to chaotic darkness like a crack house in his mind, Paul filled his thoughts with his calling to the glory of his LORD and Savior Jesus Christ. Let's take a moment to explore the concept of the mind becoming a crack house if we fail to forget negative past experiences. A crack house is where a person can obtain a quick fix and hang out to ride out their drug-induced trip. The crack house becomes a haven for desperate addicts; a den where they can find drugs, enjoy drugs, and share the experience with others, people who assist and join them in feeding their addiction.

The same thing can occur in our minds, creating a haven like a person addicted to crack cocaine. Our minds become the hangout, the go-to place we must visit for our fix. The drug of choice, or crack, for us is the painful past filled or dotted with difficult memories, baggage we have been unable to put down. Therefore, to perpetuate an unconscious self-destructive pattern, we infuse our thoughts with memories of our past, supporting our addiction by rehashing and reliving the painful experiences of yesterday. The activity that seemingly intensifies this 'high' is when we share our stories with others. Common tendency is to find as many people as we can who will allow us to share our memories, support our addiction, and validate to our pain.

Once the vicious cycle has begun and we are unaware that our painful memories have become an addiction, we are trapped without the ability to escape; just like an addict, unable to walk away. It may seem a stretch for some people to draw an association between rehashing painful memories and drug addiction, until you recognize you are unable to stop, or you recall someone who currently walks out this habit in their own lives.

The problem exists when we believe we are trying to break free from the addiction yet continue to revisit the crack houses of our minds and find others to support this dangerous habit. The very memories we claim to hinder are the memories we keep alive day after day. Paul had enough wisdom not to allow his mind to become his enemy, because once this happens, the irony is, you cannot escape from yourself. This same Paul went from persecuting Christians to proclaiming Christ and from seeking to murder Christians to ministering for Christ. He referred to himself as "the chief of all sinners" (1 Tim 1:15).

Given his past, Paul had to redirect his thoughts and give his mind a new high that would fill his life with pleasure because he was working God's calling. For Paul to serve freely, he had to successfully fill his mind with Christ-centered thoughts that served to keep his calling always before him. This behavior allowed Paul to block out memories that would preclude him from serving Christ with his whole heart. Paul refused to allow the demons of his past to haunt his mind and hinder his servanthood to God. This is the path to freedom from our past.

Paul truly understood something very few ever learn to understand. If we leave our past unresolved, those memories can become dangerous addictions that disrupt our waking moments, bombarding our thoughts and leaving us to fight a battle we are subject to lose. But you do not have to allow your mind to become your battlefield. A place where you lose every war and relive every battle. Whether you realize it or not, we all have an enemy we are fighting, an enemy with desires to "kill, steal, and destroy" (John 10:10 ESV), our future. The most amazing reason our enemy is such a formidable opponent and dangerous foe is that the tactical scheme used against us is soliciting our aide in the attack against our own souls. Follow the logic. The enemy of our soul is also the enemy of our mind, and this enemy uses *our help* to attack our mind, hoping to destroy us emotionally, physically, and spiritually.

Just how does the enemy work this strategy? By turning you against God, your support group, and finally, yourself. The attack is subtle because we are unaware of being in a fight since the enemy has us busy facing an army of perceived challenges instead. The first line of attack is from the inside out, by infiltrating our thoughts and poisoning our logic. The problem is we are totally unaware of our complicity and accuse everyone else of being off base in their thinking towards us. Take an addict, for instance; an addict's only desire is to obtain their next fix. If you help an addict fund their addiction and provide them with the drug they need to get high, you are perceived as a friend, an ally. However, anyone who tries to prevent an addict from obtaining their next fix is a perceived enemy who must be avoided, if not expelled from their inner circle. The person trying to help the addict is ironically perceived as a threat.

This is the reason why addicts often steal from close friends and family. They need to fund their next high. Nothing and no one matter to them, except the drug that has now become the one friend they crave and trust. Do you see how twisted the mind becomes? The toxic drug that is surely killing them has now become a supposed friend they turn to, and they have decided they cannot count on anyone else. Thus, the people who actually care have become dreaded threats, opponents to the deadly lifestyle the addict will do anything to protect and continue.

This same strategy causes us to abandon all forms of rational thinking, true friendships, family, and eventually, God. Listen, friend, you can't defeat this type of enemy by yourself! You have become the enemy's secret agent, solicited to destroy, well, YOU. You see, the enemy that seeks to destroy our future, by destroying our body, is the same enemy of our minds. Our minds are the primary target, and the enemy engages us and deceives us into playing something similar to Russian Roulette; I refer to this as psychological roulette.

In this game of psychological roulette, there are no bullets or guns; only thoughts, memories, and words, all associated with our past. The premise behind this vicious, self-inflicting spiral is that our mouth becomes a weapon like a gun while our thoughts and memories operate as bullets. Each time we open our mouth to "share" with others the toxic snippets from our past, we are spinning the cylinder of the gun, pulling the trigger, and firing at ourselves. Every time we revisit toxic snippets, we are closer to exposing a dangerous trigger or finally saying the one thing that could push us over the edge. This seemingly innocent practice of sharing in conversation is nothing more than emotional roulette. It can easily poison our mind, embitter our heart, and cause us to turn against our support system, ourselves, and God. The unfortunate reality is there are no winners; everyone around us loses because of our own destructive behavior.

In Psalm 13, David, the author, provides the perfect illustration of what happens when we allow our own venting to give way to sorrow.

"How long must I wrestle with my thoughts and day after day have sorrow in my heart? How long will my enemy triumph over me?" (Psalm 13:2 ESV) One of the worst outcomes of living day after day with toxic thoughts is that we eventually poison our own hearts. You do know the one person you cannot flee from is yourself, right? Resultant to this simple, yet profound reality is the fact we become deadly mirror snipers, taking aim at our own hearts with lethal self-made bullets, flying from our own mouths.

The psalmist described this struggle as a "no holds barred" wrestling match. This is where the opponents are free to use any tactics to win and the last one standing emerges victorious. The sad truth is you and your thoughts are the only opponents, and the ring is your mind. To his dismay, the psalmist at some point finally realized the wrestling match he was involved in had no time limit, adding to the grief and despair he felt deep within his heart. We become embattled in a series of matches we cannot win, because we are our own opponent.

The Bible clearly warns us to beware of the "schemes of the devil" (Ephesians 6:11 ESV), because they are many. That is the point, we are up against a crafty enemy that will use diverse tactics to control us for the purpose of ultimately destroying us. Don't be deceived!

The behavior mentioned before is easy to spot in others, but difficult to identify in oneself, partly because operating in negativity is a new way of life. We all know individuals who tend to only critique and criticize everything and everybody, drawing the most dire and grim conclusions. Rarely do they have something good to say about anyone or anything. They always have a problem to report, or a situation that feeds anguish and drama. Very seldom do they report good news. If they happen to slip out some good news, a bad report is sure to follow close behind. These people have perfected the art of turning lemonade back into lemons. Every conversation becomes an opportunity to manipulate and control the narrative, to talk about something negative that once happened to them. They frequently hijack conversations with a timely: "You know, that same thing happened to me...", or "I remember when I...", "Be careful. I know about that all too well." If you try to redirect them or call out their negative behavior patterns, they will simply find someone else who will allow them to vent and share.

Your ears are no longer needed. You have violated your agreement to allow them to vomit their toxic conversations all over you. Unfortunately, these people have no idea that each time they share, they are poisoning themselves with their own words. This type of mindset and negative thinking has become a way of life that is not easy to resist or let go of. If you have ever dealt with this type of behavioral issue in others, you must have witnessed how they cleverly drag painful memories along as they move down life's journey. This self-destructive pattern has become so prevalent in their lives that they are literally blind to their actions, making an emotional transition or healthy relationship of any kind almost impossible. Strife and confrontation can wreak havoc on even the closest relationships, especially when others try to show the troubled person the error of their ways. Everyone who tries to help is typically met with angry, emotional outbursts, or words that express, "You just don't understand," when essentially, they are the ones who have failed to grasp a level of understanding that reveals need for help.

Behavior like this generally leads to choking bitterness over their past. This bitterness causes resentment toward self, toward others, toward life, and even resentment toward God. If they once had faith, that faith tends to diminish in a struggle to believe God cares, a struggle to understand how God could love them and still allow them to go through such painful experiences. This reality is too hard for some to accept. They simply grow more bitter and instead of embracing God or accepting any accountability for their own choices and actions, many accuse God of mishandling their lives.

Although some people search for answers the best way they know how, they have chosen the wrong path by calling God's sovereignty into question, and failing to identify the real enemy. Therefore, God becomes the enemy. God takes the hit since His sovereignty allows Him complete autonomy to control every situation, and the ability to know all before any good or bad situation transpires. Therefore, He becomes the ultimate recipient of all blame because He did not edit the outcome in their favor. The situation went wrong on His watch. A person of a certain mindset thinks to themself:

"God allowed this to happen."

"People mistreated me. God could have stopped this from occurring before they hurt me."

"God could have prevented me from this life-altering mistake since he knew I was going to eventually make that wrong decision."

A hurting person allows all the blame to point back to God. Powerful negative thought progressions have led them down the worst path imaginable, finding an enemy in God. Resentment and bitterness have become the secret sauce that brews in their heart and mind, poisoning them against God. Their perception of Him has soured and trust in God has been destroyed. They pray, but the content of their prayers has descended into doubt, whining, and accusations against the very God that is able to deliver them.

See, the definition of God's goodness has become tainted with expectations of God's performance, His response to the secret demands cloaked in what they call prayer. When God does not meet those selfish demands of the corrupted heart and mind, He is no longer considered good. This conveniently offers God as a scapegoat, justification for anger and continued resentment towards Him. This, my friend, is the colossal mistake of allowing the root of bitterness to fester, resulting in disillusionment and distance between the suffering person and salvation.

Unfortunately, it is precisely when God is needed most that the increasingly confused mind and hardening heart has driven Him farther away. This dismal pattern of behavior and subsequent outcomes is difficult to rebound from, since people who operate this way are unlikely to recognize, relent, or change despite sound persuasion or even Biblical wisdom. Their hearts and minds are both feeding on the same internal coffer of poison. If you ever had trouble encouraging someone, the reason is they constantly fuel the poison of their own negative thoughts rather than eat from the hand offering encouraging food. They are unable to see or accept what forces them to forget the pain of their past and try to move on.

Since you cannot argue against the pain of someone's past, you cannot convince them that it is the origin of their cycle of self-abuse. Of course, the longer the behavior persists, the more they become jaded by their thoughts and potential for helping them recover becomes more and more implausible. And yet, let me pause to say, all hope is not lost. God is "able to make all *grace to abound...*" towards them (2 Cor 9:8 ESV).

Regrettably, the ultimate trip hazard that causes man to stumble is failing to perceive that God is always good, even if our thoughts of God are not always good.

"How do we keep from falling apart when our world begins to unravel? That's what we all want to know. The answer is simple and profound: We need to tenaciously praise God. Even in the midst of turmoil, we can choose to be "wounded worshippers." Praising God can get you through even the toughest of times."[3]

If we could somehow evaluate our own failure to properly honor God, purely because He is deserving of our most fruitful praise, we would eventually discover the freedom that accompanies praise delivered up to God and God alone. This is the freedom that can eventually bury unholy thoughts and feelings toward God, giving birth to a new heart filled with praise, and a mind stayed on Him. I think we can safely conclude that the Apostle Paul understood the proverbial boomerang effect caused by praising God, so he continually encouraged—no, beseeched us, to rejoice. Rejoice not in events, happy occasions, or fleeting moments, but to rejoice in the LORD. One step towards freedom.

The Practice of Idolizing Our Past

I respectfully suggest paying close, careful attention to what you are about to read. Believe it or not, we all have the ability to create idols. It is easy to develop an unhealthy and unholy habit of idol worship. As we may or may not know, God understands full well the condition of our hearts and the need for man to worship, so he dedicated a commandment to help us steer clear of this dreadful practice. "Do not have any other Gods besides me." (Exodus 20:3 ESV)

Acting as if this command no longer applies, or was meant for another time and people, is the slippery slope that slides us right into the idols of our past. The word idol can refer to "an image or representation of a god-thing used as an object of worship." Likewise, worship refers to "paying honor or homage out of reverence toward something or someone." Therefore, idol worship is paying reverence, honoring something or someone other than God.

When we devote constant attention toward the pain and disappointment of failing to achieve some desire, goal or dream, we essentially erect a mental idol of the painful experience, directing undeserved energy to our past. It may start out by simply sharing feelings with a close family member, friend, or associate. Then it becomes constantly discussing the memory on a regular basis. This practice is rationally defended by suggesting we are simply trying to come to grips with the trauma, or trying to make some sense out of what occurred. This is genuine and honest in early stages of reflection and processing.

However, days turn into months and months turn into years before we are caught up still discussing the same moments of anguish, only now reciting more and more details as we go along. Once challenged by our family and friends to cease discussing the same events repeatedly, we may find ourselves embarrassed, thus offering, "This is the last time I am going to bring this up." The truth is, we literally lose count of how many times we have made those meaningless promises to drop it and let it go. What we don't realize is this practice has become a highly sustainable habit that feeds on itself. We are now unable to effectively break from it because we have walked in this behavior for way too long. We have successfully given our past the right to coexist with us as an idol.

How does this happen? One might dare to ask. It's simple, I suppose. If you spend an enormous amount of time rehashing any one subject, you keep not only the memory alive, but the pain remains as well. Do you see this?

Now, ask yourself why would you let yourself to continue to suffer like this if the pain of the experience no longer serves any positive or productive purpose? Why continue to remind yourself of the trauma by revisiting all the details every time you find someone who will listen? This is blatant idol worship. Your past has become your idol and your mind is unfortunately the sacrifice. You rob yourself of embracing any positive people, places, and activities because you are stuck in some distant moment of toxic trauma, going over it again and again. As you constantly pay homage to your painful past, you forfeit precious peace of mind in the present.

I only hope by reading this you will come to grips with what you are doing or have done to your own mental wellness. You are literally robbing yourself of moments of joy and happiness that are rightfully yours, all because you are dwelling to keep your most difficult life moments alive and well. This self-inflicted suffering only serves to make you a martyr in your own eyes. Pay careful attention, my friend. You cannot continue to live this way if you desire to achieve inner peace and contentment.

Continuing to discuss the past year in and year out only works to demotivate, deplete energy, drown out inner peace, and destroy any sense of hope. There is no wonder why many suffer from bouts of depression and mood swings. An unwittingly created toxic environment has poisoned mind, heart, and soul. People overdose on the pain of their past, seeking each fix like a junkie needing endless repetition and review, no longer seeking relief so much as any opportunity to spew horrors of the past to anyone who will listen.

Don't misunderstand me; none of this is meant to shame anyone; only to warn you to wake up before your mind is no longer willing or able to function in your favor. Stop treating your thoughts like a hazardous waste dump. The mind can only take in so many toxins before mental illness takes hold. No, this book is not a treatise on mental health, nor I am the second coming of Dr. Freud. I am simply a person who cares enough to warn you that you cannot continue to treat yourself this way. You deserve better.

I understand that the required self-awareness isn't always present to protect you from yourself. It is possible you had no idea of the mistreatment and punishment you've been inflicting on yourself, perhaps until you started reading this book. My hope is that once you have read each section of this book you will start to allow yourself room to heal, you will recognize the counter-productive destruction you've caused, and you will find a way to move on with your life, free and unburdened. I hope you will find the strength to tear down the idols of your past and worship the only one who deserves our worship, the Almighty God.

The Idol of Regret: Live forward without being shackled by regrets

Regret can consume the best of us, primarily due to the fact that we erect a throne for our regrets that we visit often over the course of our lives. You see, regret by itself is not as problematic as one might suppose. The term itself means remorse or repentance. Certainly, remorse is a normal reaction for any decent human being if they have contributed to something that went wrong.

The term 'repentance' also carries a healthy perspective; one that should emerge from within us once we determine our actions or behavior have missed the mark. Obviously, neither of these words carry negative connotations, nor is showing and displaying remorse or repentance a bad behavior. From God's perspective, His Holy word encourages us to have a heart of repentance. Thus, we find, "Repent therefore, and turn back, that your sins may be blotted out, that times of refreshing may come from the presence of the Lord, and that he may send the Christ appointed for you, Jesus." (Acts 3:19-20 ESV).

As you can see, repentance is a positive behavior that leads to a healing and rewarding experience. What causes regret to turn sour is when we allow the memory of the regretful situation to consume us. This is the practice that must stop. The way to escape this unhealthy pattern is to accept that we all have regrets in our past, things we wish had been different, but we can no longer change. However, this does not require self-inflicting punishment for something you cannot reverse.

Stop punishing yourself with the dagger of regret when you cannot undo what has already been done. The best approach is to learn from the mistake and move on. No matter how much you feel a mistake has cost you, no matter how lasting the consequence, just move on. Living with perpetual focus on regret is a draining and discouraging behavior that will eventually erode positive energy and threaten an otherwise successful life.

Many people walk around blaming some mistake they made years ago for their lack of success, but the truth is that mistake did not paralyze their ability to live a successful life, the paralysis resulted from living with and worshiping the idol of regret. "It's not what happens to you, but how you respond that really matters."[4] When we learn to fully grasp this concept, we increase our ability to live forward without being shackled to and by our regrets.

The Idol of Past Mistakes: Use Mistakes to Change the Course of Someone's Life

Given certain circumstances and the magnitude of corresponding consequences, the past can, and will, haunt you. I will not deny the potential of a mistake having staying power to disrupt your steps and potentially trip you up in the future. Past mistakes can easily trip up your mind and disrupt your emotional well-being. This disruption is emotional trauma that can persist for years without respite. I am fully aware of the suffering people go through, dealing with some experience of their yesterday that affects their today and tomorrows.

This is not meant to minimize the circumstances and consequences we face as a result of our past. On the contrary, this chapter is meant to shed light on how to escape the self-imposed, self-destructive behavior of making your mistakes into idols. We have already covered the dangers of allowing our regrets to become idols. It is essential to also address the catalyst that sets this in motion, so we can find the right formula to prevent this regrettable cause and effect.

Follow this chain reaction with me, if you please. Let's say you take your parents' car at the age of 13 and go for a joy ride, causing thousands of dollars in damage because you end up in a serious accident. You earned yourself a juvenile record because this was not your first brush with the law. Due to the amount of damage you caused, the judge insists you need to learn a lesson. Once you have grown up, some years later, you decide to change your undisciplined ways and walk the straight and narrow. However, even though you have learned from your past mistakes, your record keeps coming up whenever you try to apply for a job. Consequences have taken root and you can't seem to shake the result of your youthful folly.

Your past has now started to hinder your future. Aspirations feel unattainable and you grow more frustrated, believing yourself a victim, blaming the system, with seemingly no way out. The frustration is real, your problems are real, and the closed doors are all too real. But, as real as these hurdles are, you must fight to avoid turning your past mistake into an idol. Just because the past is causing you some delays and setbacks, this does not justify giving up or bowing out of the race. We must hold steady, stay focused, continue to try and succeed.

When you find yourself endlessly rehashing, 'worshiping' your regret and letting it become an 'idol' will only cause sleepless nights, unrealized dreams, and too many wasted moments to count. I am writing this book with good news! There is a choice. The path behind us is finished, it can no longer be helped. But the path in front of us is ours to choose. I want everyone reading this right now to realize that we all have the power to choose our way forward. Develop a prayerful plan of action and develop it now. To continue living without a plan potentially leads to emotional distress. It is too easy to get stuck in a cycle feeling trapped, internalizing a reality that we believe cannot change. I am here to tell you, my friend, that you cannot undo your past, turn back the hands of time, or throw away hours, days, weeks, months, YEARS wishing your life turned out differently. Instead, we must spend our precious time making positive strides to succeed DESPITE our past. *Don't waste your pain.* Recognize the power within when we turn to prayer and develop a plan of action.

Years ago, upon graduating from college, I was unable to land a job in my field of study. I had no work experience, and I possessed a degree that I was told was no longer, "the recruiter's choice." The deck seemed stacked against me. What was a graduate to do? Let me be honest, I felt defeated. I couldn't celebrate my win (finishing college) because I was busy trying to overcome not being able to land my first job as a graduate. Did I feel like giving up? Of course I did. I was upset, confused, and bewildered with the whole process.

Finally, after a few months of beating my head against that wall, I chose an action plan. I chose to enroll in school, and tried to gain some work experience through an internship. Little did I know then, God had an alternative plan for me, and I believe this plan only came to fruition because I chose to take action and develop a plan.

The rest is history. I went back to school, enrolled in FAMU/FSU College of Engineering, and earned my degree in Electrical Engineering. I have enjoyed a prosperous career that almost never happened, had I given up. Although God stepped in and worked a different path to mine, at least I gave him something to work with. Do you follow me?

The risk of continuing on a destructive course is it fosters an emotionally unstable state of mind, with past mistakes always precluding you from moving forward. Doors close, dreams seem dashed, opportunities fade. Consequently, you establish a pattern of frequently worshipping those regrets, which becomes the main cause for paralysis.

How do you know if you have a problem with worshipping your past? What does worship look like from this perspective? We can describe the behavior of worship as physically and inwardly bowing down and submitting out of a willingness to serve, giving honor to something or someone. Therefore, to worship your past is to credit your mistakes as controlling agents of your life's outcome, moments of history that you consider worthy of honoring for the duration of your life. Worshipping your past suggests that God's veto power is limited in dictating the outcome of your future, incapable of righting any wrongs you have committed.

Well, allow me to offer "hoping hand" that many are unable to find on their own. Instead of surrendering to ghosts of the past, let frustration fuel your desire to change the course of your future. The truth is we cannot undo our past no matter how long we wish our mistakes away. However, there is something you can achieve despite the dark clouds precipitated by regret. You can learn from your past and help others avoid the same mistakes. Learning new behavior not only frees you, but gives new purpose to the past. Bad choices and missteps are not wasted because we can turn mistakes into a platform to help others. I dare anyone to try this plan of action! I challenge you to help someone else avoid your same pitfalls. Change the narrative of your conversation and give your pain a mission.

You will discover there are plenty of opportunities to use the events of your personal history to help others along their journey. For instance, the person who established a nonprofit organization to help at-risk youth because they spent their teen years making wrong decisions and wasting precious time. The generations of reformed young adults in that organization have tried to help steer others in the right direction before they fall prey to the same traps they fell prey to.

In what way could you help someone by sharing your time and experience? How could you make a difference by helping others make better choices, increasing their chances to succeed? Imagine how great it would feel to change the course of someone's life because of caring enough to share lessons learned and teach rather than resent your past. Time to make a difference, time to try.

The Idol of Mimicking Mistakes of Others: Break the Cycle

One of the oddest discoveries in life is that we tend to mimic our parents' and guardians' behavior. This includes their weaknesses and mistakes at least as much as their strengths and successes. Can you relate? Even when we tell ourselves, "I am not going to make the mistakes my parents made," ironically, we somehow open the same doors and walk the same yellow brick roads they traveled, leading to similar, if not the very same results our parents and guardians faced.

For instance—interpersonal relationships, familial or otherwise. When parents struggle with relationships inside and outside the home, children tend to adopt the same struggles in their own lives. Parental modeling becomes ingrained in our minds; unconsciously infused into our interpersonal rhythms and played out through our own behavior. As hard as we try to fight against repeating their patterns, we subconsciously become our parents. God forbid they divorced or had addictions they succumbed to in their lifetime, where, as season ticket holders we had front row seats as we were growing up.

No one sets out to imitate our parents' failures; we simply learn to model behaviors we are most familiar with and accustomed to seeing. In relationships, this can be destructive because others are unaware of any dark side developed by our past. Our children, spouses, and other unsuspecting people become innocent victims because wounded people tend to wound others. Before long, relationships struggle and suffer greatly because we are unaware of lasting emotional trauma from dysfunctional parental engagements.

Sometimes the issues our parents passed along play such a role in our own development, we find ourselves ill-equipped to carry on a meaningful relationship. Relationships require maintenance, being unselfish, giving, forgiving, loving, peaceful, and not lawbreaking or risk-taking. Healthy bonds with people require listening, understanding, and being emotionally in control rather than confrontational. It isn't productive or kind to constantly take the battlefield for the slightest misunderstanding. Relationships need a healing touch, not reaching for weapons (verbal or otherwise) simply because we cannot have our way or don't like the way things are going.

Now, this is not meant to criticize our parents. They too came from dysfunctional environments, hence the dysfunctional behavior they modeled in front of us. The point is, we need to recognize this cycle and ascertain the effects on us, take steps to emotionally heal, and break the cycle for good. The cycle can be broken. This however will only occur when we stop living in denial and avoiding reality. We must recognize and own that our past can explain us, but *does not* excuse us from being accountable for our own behavior. Our past does not absolve us from who we have allowed ourselves to become. We must admit we suffered, acknowledge we are still in pain, and seek or develop the right tools to skillfully conduct ourselves in meaningful relationships.

Once we openly and honestly admit to our own undeniable truths, then we must seek personal help for ourselves. You see, our relationships suffer because we never resolved hurt and pain from before. Therefore, we need first and foremost to seek help. We should never use current relationships as a cop-out to avoid reflection and healing. This will only delay and camouflage the real problem—that we have been emotionally scarred, and that scarring becomes a source of tension and conflict that wreaks havoc until it is resolved.

Unfortunately, parental or familial dysfunction can also trigger overwhelming insecurities that lead us to doubt our partner's commitment. We question love for us and mistrust rather than seeing we are the ones destroying the growth, closeness, and intimacy we long for in our relationships. Unwittingly our callous behavior sets in motion a self-fulfilling prophesy that leads to failed marriages and endless cycles of broken relationships. This is more disturbing because most victimizers don't set out to behave this way. However, once they start using those dysfunctional muscles developed by the steroids of parental modeling, they are unable to turn this behavior off and blindly become the Hulk in their relationships.

You remember the Hulk, don't you? The Hulk's alter ego was a mild-mannered individual, one of the nicest people you could meet. Sound familiar? However, when pushed into a corner or engaged in the slightest confrontation, this mild-mannered person becomes an uncontrollable, destructive green giant. Now, I am not suggesting you are the Hulk, dear reader, because he is a simply a cartoon character. I am however trying to paint a clear illustration of what takes place when there is a darkness lurking inside. When you fail to resolve parental dysfunction from your youth, it develops into your own dysfunction, woven into your character.

What should you do? Seek help, people! You deserve to recognize, process, and overcome this for yourself. Your family deserves for you to be well and wholly present, right now today, not trapped by trauma or dysfunction in your past. Stop living in constant denial and blaming others for your failed relationships. Turn your life around so you can have meaningful bonds that are warm, welcoming, reciprocating, and fruitful. Relationships where you can live in peace and harmony even when you don't always walk in agreement. What a wonderful opportunity awaits if you would just take that first step to healing, admitting you need help.

Yes, our parents played a pivotal role in our formative years, but we need not blame them to move forward. We need only to identify the triggers so we can grow and engage without fear of the Hulk appearing on the scene; so we can potentially walk in better relationships with everyone we encounter.

Chapter 2

The Idol of Missed Opportunities: Never Abandon God

The Painful Experience

2 Samuel 12:16-23 English Standard Version (ESV)

16 David therefore sought God on behalf of the child. And David fasted and went in and lay all night on the ground. 17 And the elders of his house stood beside him, to raise him from the ground, but he would not, nor did he eat food with them. 18 On the seventh day the child died. And the servants of David were afraid to tell him that the child was dead, for they said, "Behold, while the child was yet alive, we spoke to him, and he did not listen to us. How then can we say to him the child is dead? He may do himself some harm." 19 But when David saw that his servants were whispering together, David understood that the child was dead. And David said to his servants, "Is the child dead?" They said, "He is dead." 20 Then David arose from the earth and washed and anointed himself and changed his clothes. And he went into the house of the Lord and worshiped. He then went to his own house. And when he asked, they set food before him,

and he ate. 21 Then his servants said to him, "What is this thing that you have done? You fasted and wept for the child while he was alive; but when the child died, you arose and ate food." 22 He said, "While the child was still alive, I fasted and wept, for I said, 'Who knows whether the Lord will be gracious to me, that the child may live?' 23 But now he is dead. Why should I fast? Can I bring him back again? I shall go to him, but he will not return to me."

We are often reminded that losing a child is one of the most trying experiences a person can face. These experiences are often described as "a part of me died," or "a void that can never be filled." The behavior of King David in this passage of scripture cosigns this sentiment expressed by many who have grieved the passing of a child, nevertheless this passage also reveals much more to us if we examine the text carefully.

While David's child was near death, he solemnly threw himself at the mercy of God in hope that God would grant him favor. King David abandoned his normal routine behavior of eating and drinking, and even resting in the comfort of his own bed, while his child was near death. Although stricken with grief over what could eventually happen, David's strategy was simple: appeal to God while there is still room for hope. David hoped in the Lord.

Take notice of what David did and the behavior he did not exhibit during his time of suffering. When David's newborn baby took ill, verse 16 tells us that David turned to God on behalf of his child, hoping God would intervene. David turned to the only one who was able to make a difference in his dire situation. Notice, he did not throw blame at God or abandon his faith in God during his ordeal.

This should serve as a powerful lesson for us to learn. David did not turn against God or blame God for the child's sickness. Instead, he sought the LORD for his mercy through fasting, revealing his perspective of the LORD, his reverential heart toward the Almighty God. This story is a reminder that we are not to think it strange when we go through trying ordeals in our lives. Even when we are facing inevitable trials, we may start to feel like trouble knows our address by heart. To make matters worse, we sometimes feel as though trouble has personally started sending gift-wrapped pain to our front door. If this is how you feel, allow this story to provide a consistent reminder that there is enough trouble in life to go around for us all.

None of us will leave this earth without experiencing our fair share of trouble, either directly or indirectly. Because of this one fact, there are a plethora of lessons we can learn from the way David chose to behave during a dreadful nightmare of a trial. In short, he took his cares to God, petitioned God for favor, and when God said no to his request, he didn't abandon his faith in God. Do yourself a favor and pay careful attention to the significance of David's behavior. <u>Never abandon God</u>.

Idolizing the Villains of Our Past: Release the Villains and Live

One factor that confounds painful experiences of our past is vivid recall of the roles different villains played. These villains become ingrained in our memory banks, only to win Emmys for their roles in our pain each time we tell our stories. Because we allow those villains to continue playing their roles actively in our minds, the pain of the memory remains as active and painful to us as if the event happened yesterday. By preserving the villains, we preserve the pain. By releasing the villains of our story through forgiveness, we aid in releasing ourselves from the pain. As long as we maintain mental contact with our villains, we delay our release and deny ourselves much needed distance from the traumatic experience. Oddly enough, it is rare to realize this association, and many develop a counterproductive habit of holding the villains accountable for their role in our pain rather than holding ourselves accountable for the empowerment needed to move on. We essentially deny our own emotional emancipation.

There was a man by the name of Joseph who found himself face to face one day with the villains from his past. These were the same people who played a pivotal role in separating him from his parents, causing him to grow up outside the company of his own family. The villains from his story just happened to be very close to him, his own brothers. They had so much disdain and jealousy toward him, they devised a plot to kill him, only to eventually decide to sell him into slavery instead.

Naturally, Joseph's life was never the same again. Can you imagine being robbed of growing up in your own home, with your own parents, being forced to have a totally different childhood and young adult experience? All this because your own siblings were so jealous of your potential future, they set out to change the course of your life and ruin you forever.

Don't misunderstand the point here. I am not suggesting that the villains are not guilty of whatever egregious acts they committed, and I am not suggesting the ordeal suffered didn't have a significant impact on that time in your life. On the contrary, I am suggesting that your current feelings toward the villains are unequivocally causing you more harm than you realize. Do yourself a favor and if you desire to heal, move forward without carrying the pain of your past any further into the future. Learn to practice forgiveness for your own sake. That is the path to release. Now I understand if this were easy, most would choose to make this happen. Therefore, I would like to provide you with several reasons to jump start your forgiveness potential.

One elementary reason is that the people you are holding grudges, animosity, and hatred toward more than likely do not even recall what you are so disturbed about in the first place. When people hurt others, they rarely sit around dwelling on what they did to their victims. They might not know how badly they hurt you, or so much time has lapsed between events, they have forgotten the ordeal, and possibly even you. Yet there you are, suffering while they have moved on with their lives.

The second reason is more important than the first. Jesus told his disciples, "If you do not forgive others their trespasses, neither will your Father forgive your trespasses." (Matthew 6:15 ESV) Remember I stated earlier how Joseph came face to face with his villains? Well, what do you think Joseph did when this occurred? Do you think he blasted his brothers for robbing him of his chance to grow up with his parents, to watch his parents grow older, to have a chance at a normal life?

Joseph practiced the very act necessary to break free from pain of the past by setting his heinous villains free. When Joseph came face to face with his brothers, this is how he handled the situation. In Genesis Chapter 50, verse 20, Joseph spoke these often-recited words in Christian circles: "As for you, you meant evil against me, but God meant it for good, to bring it about that many people should be kept alive, as they are today."

Joseph's response to his brothers provides the proper path toward releasing both villain and victim (self), from crippling memories that bind the two parties together. This is significant because after being mistreated by his brothers and sold into slavery to the Egyptians, he rose to prominence as second in command only to Pharaoh. When he saw his brothers again, Joseph was in a position of power where he could have easily exacted revenge for the pain they inflicted on him many years before. Yet, instead of using his power to seek revenge—as some of us might think to do—Joseph saw the hand and plan of God in his ordeal, rather than the malpractice of man.

As we observe Joseph's address to the people that played a major role in altering his life forever, he absolves them of their responsibility and releases them from condemnation by crediting God with being ultimately in control. Notice, he did not condone their behavior. On the contrary, he clearly asserted that their actions against him were nothing short of evil, showing that Joseph did recall exactly what happened to him by the hands of his villains, yet he was able to move on without feeling obligated to "repay evil for evil" (1 Peter 3:9 ESV).

Joseph knew his perpetrators, recalled the pain of his past, recognized the evil acts committed against him by his villainous brothers, and still asserted God's sovereignty. Amazing! How many of us would exonerate those who deliberately damaged us? *The answer is probably, not many. Unlike Joseph, we wouldn't credit God's involvement because we wouldn't see a purpose for our ordeal.*

Joseph was able to discredit his brothers' plan of evil and credit God's sovereign ability to guide the course of his life. By seeing the hand and plan of God, Joseph was able to remove the bitterness towards his brothers, releasing them and himself from his painful, unfair past. This avoids the stumbling block of haunting memories that cripple us when we are unable to let go. Joseph did not waste his pain.

All too often we become so fixated on the people responsible for inflicting our pain we never fathom God ability to bless us through our ordeal. Focusing on the perpetrators not only blinds us from seeing what God is able to do with our trial; this can also place us in bondage to the trial. Joseph was able to channel his focus on God by realizing a sovereign God can use the worst most painful experience to advance his plan and purpose in the lives of others. This serves as proof we should look to God during our painful moments and seek his purpose for our pain.

We never know when God is up to something. Granted, we would rather escape this life without experiencing dark moments, but it is comforting to know our pain does not have to be in vain, that our suffering can one day become a blessing. That makes life even more worth living, because no one will escape even the disappointments that life brings, either through the hands of others or our own hands. For all these reasons, we can all take a page from Joseph's book on living life forward.

The Idol of Failed Goals: Do Not Allow Your Goals to Represent Your Treasure

Goals are important place holders that motivate us to accomplish our dreams. There are times when we fall short of accomplishing the objectives we set for ourselves, and depending on the cause of any setback, this can cause severe and lasting emotional trauma. We are raised to set goals and plan for our futures, and those goals become closely tied to our self-esteem. However, rarely are we coached to develop backup plans and coping skills for when our goals fail to come to fruition. Consequently, we are not prepared for life's disappointments. When they happen, we suffer a first-round knockout and struggle to recover for the rest of life's fight.

Even though goals carry significance, we cannot allow them to consume our life or become our only hope for the future. A boxer goes into the ring having prepared for the fight with a single plan in mind. However, once the first round begins, the plan may or may not work depending on the boxer's opponent. Nevertheless, experienced boxers with experienced corner-men, are able to adjust and adapt to counterattack their opponent.

Well, life is somewhat of a boxing match, even for those of us who never enter the ring. We set goals or fight plans only to experience unexpected struggles from life's opponents, leading to knock downs or serious body punches that can be overwhelming. To recover and win, we must have the flexibility to keep going rather than being crushed by the unexpected setback. This is the danger of not having a backup plan.

Goals were never meant to become our idols; something we worship with our hearts, minds, and souls. Goals should simply keep us in perpetual motion, desiring the best for our future as we consistently maneuver with hope of personal success. Goals should never prematurely become realized achievements in our minds. A completed vision of mission accomplished can be a powerful fantasy that is hard to let go of, and if we fail to reach a desired goal, we get stuck, unable to turn the corner and keep striving. So, what should we do if we have already made this mistake? Simple. Develop and work your Plan B, C, or D. Adjust. Adapt. Never give up. Keep the faith. Continue to live forward.

The unfortunate reality is very few of us are able to transition to Plan B mode. Not that we don't want to, or somewhat realize we need to; we just can't seem to make the shift. I suggest that the reason for inability to shift is because we have made our desired goal the object of our affection instead of something to achieve. The Bible raises this warning in Matthew Chapter 6, verse 21, "For where your treasure is, there your heart will be also."

In one of the most profound addresses known in scripture, as the "Sermon on the Mount", Jesus provided several instructions to his disciples concerning worldly-minded consumption that poisons our perspective on life. In verse 21 of Chapter 6, he warns them of allowing their hearts to become corrupted by misplaced affection on earthly treasures. The reason for the warning is clear: our hearts are easily seduced by temptations once we have chosen the object of our affection. Therefore, we must use wisdom and discernment to make our selections and avoid digging for meaningless treasure. This warning aptly applies to placing too much emphasis on achieving lifelong goals instead of moving forward when we come up short. When we establish goals, remain objective, and realize that everything we set out to achieve may not come to fruition, we are better equipped to pivot and overcome, to keep living without being stuck and unable to get out of our own way.

Some of the best running backs in the National Football League are not necessarily the players that break long runs each time they carry the ball. Instead, the best running backs (in my humble opinion) are the players that fight through the initial hit from the opposing tackler only to fall forward when they are falling. If this isn't clear, let me elucidate the point: The opponent puts a solid hit on the running back; they are hit hard and eventually tackled by more opponents, but despite the hard hit, the running back is still able to fall forward for positive yards, which I now refer to as yards after contact (YAC).

What's your YAC total? What's your yearning after contact, when life knocks you down? Do you fall forward after the initial hit, or set back? Are you able to continue to gain positive emotional yards after life puts a hard hit on you? Do you struggle through the hit as best you can, determined to make positive strides no matter the circumstances? See, running backs know their opponents are going to hit them and try to deliver a vicious tackle each time they carry the ball.

Even though the goal for the ball carrier is to run for a touchdown every down, the reality is they are going to take hits during the game. The success of the running back depends more on their ability to fight through the hits and gain as many yards as possible after contact. If you think I am promoting football, you've missed the point. Although our desire is to run through life achieving our set goals, life will invariably put a hit on us and take us down short of our intended goal line.

Suffered through a divorce? Knocked to the ground. Lost your job? Knocked to the ground. Failed a major test or nearly flunked out of school? Knocked down again. Lost your home and forced to move around, trying to find housing? Another blow. Struggling with a chronic illness? The hits keep coming. These are only a few examples of being tackled by life. Our success after contact depends on whether we fall forward or backward. Do we rise and push on, or wallow in self-pity? How will you fall when you receive your next hit?

The Dream That Never Materialized

We've covered that a well-developed Plan B can help us live drama-free as we navigate life's journey. Surprisingly enough, very few people acknowledge or act on the necessity of developing a Plan B. I believe this is because we see living this way as a suggestion that we don't have faith in ourselves or our original goals. Flexibility is too often seen as weakness rather than strength in the ability to adjust and adapt. Therefore, we sink all our eggs into one proverbial basket, hoping everything goes according to the one dream that we have nursed and cherished for years. Then, one day, something goes wrong and we come to see that the future we envisioned will not happen as we hoped.

Without an alternative plan, awareness that your dream may never come to fruition starts a chain reaction deep within that most of us are ill-equipped to handle. In fact, how many people expect life to alter their plans, unseating a prearranged course of action, throwing a curve ball we are unable to hit? The simple answer is, very few of us plan for life this way. Very few receive training on how to cope with life's most difficult moments.

What invariably happens when our future doesn't materialize according to plan is, we become emotionally distraught, sink into depression, and eventually grow angry over the disappointment. The resentment and sadness we feel eventually leads to self-pity, and a need to blame someone other than ourselves. Emotions continue to wear upon us, and without anger and blame to fuel us, we would probably implode.

However, these emotions were never meant to pave our road or provide healing salve for our pain. Instead of life becoming easier, we grow bitter as we struggle to live normally despite traumatic setbacks, continuing a downward spiral until we find comfort in throwing blame as a way of releasing frustration and anxiety. Typically, blame is placed with the only one who can help us rise above our pit of despair and find our way back to a life worth living—God Himself.

Unfortunately, throwing shade at God will never solve our problems or lift our spirits. In fact, raising anger towards God only crowds Him out and magnifies our inability to heal without His help. No wonder the Bible warns us that "for the anger of man does not produce the righteousness of God", (James 1:20 ESV). Amazing, the way we credit ourselves with our successes and castigate God for our failures. Ironically, the one we need most is the one our anger causes us to turn on, alienating us in our lowest moments.

"God is our refuge and strength, a very present help in trouble (Psalm 46:1 ESV).

I like the fact that the Bible does not merely suggest that God could help or would be willing to help if He is able to. No, this verse assures us that in God we have someone we can always count on during the most unsettling and troubling times. God is not our enemy.

Chapter 3

God is Not the Enemy

Without realizing our own irreverent actions, oftentimes we portray God as the villain that sets out to destroy our future. When we face unexpected setbacks and unacceptable disappointments, we rush to hold God responsible because He is sovereign. We determine that God should have prevented, diverted, redirected the situation to preserve our dreams and bring our goals to fruition. After all, He is all-knowing (omniscient), all-powerful (omnipotent), and everywhere (omnipresent). Simply put, God is King.

Can you discern why this perspective of God—being required to preserve our goals and dreams—is oxymoronic? Essentially, we are speaking with respect to the God of the universe being required to focus on us, to ensure we receive what we desire out of life and to make our dreams and wishes come true. *Unfortunately, this mindset turns God into a magic genie, reducing his reign into something solely for our selfish gain.*

Reducing God to some personal magic genie allows us to believe and expect that He easily could and should have stepped in to prevent us from making a mistake in the first place. Or, He could have at least diverted trouble away from us and delivered us through the problem without any lasting effect. Therefore, we conclude that the blame must rest solely on

God. This line of thinking is the catalyst that fosters idolizing our past failures. Never mind the fact that we all make mistakes. Never mind the truth that more people succeed the second time around or after a few failed attempts than the one-hit wonders who succeed on the first try.

Life is filled with disappointments, do-overs, and second chances. Everyone must face their fair share of them all, and just because you don't have a front row view of my missteps and setbacks, does not negate that they happened.

Why do we feel a need to blame God? *The answer is, we simply don't like trusting God through pain and disappointment.* We prefer to trust God only when life is going our way, when we are on top, when we don't have a care in the world; and whenever we step up to the proverbial plate, we hit a home run with every swing of the bat. That is when we shout, "I trust Him." Only during the joys of life does God seem to have earned our trust in him. This is also when we are most prone to praise Him. However, the truth is, in the absence of a test, how can you know for certain that you truly trust God? Of course, no one sits around waiting to welcome trials; however, setbacks can serve as an opportunity to display faith in God's sovereign plan.

Let's look at Job, who we are told lived long ago in the land of Uz. In fact, the Bible documents a portion of Job's adult life for us to examine by dedicating an entire book compiled of 42 Chapters in the Old Testament. In the book of Job, we find one of the most frequently quoted and provocative statements in the entire Bible. In Chapter 13, verse 15a., Job states, "Though he slay me, I will hope in him". That's how the text is recorded in the English Standard version. Can I tell you I like the King James version a little better? "Though he slay me, yet will I trust in Him."

Either rendering of this passage provides the right perspective and reverence to display toward a holy and righteous God. Without going into detail, we can ascertain how Job's words reflect a man committed to the Lord regardless of the trials in his life, the pain he felt, or the weight of the rejection he felt from concluding God was against him. Through all his suffering, Job remained committed to trusting God.

A little more insight is needed to place Job's statement in a context with relevance to our own lives. The Bible records for us in the Book of Job that one day this man Job (described as a man who lived a perfect life), had one of the most tragic experiences a person could ever imagine facing without losing their own life. All in one day, Job went from being a father of ten and the wealthiest man in his region, to fatherless and stripped of all his worldly riches. To make matters worse, shortly after these tragedies befell Job, he became gravely ill and was unable to fully resolve the loss of his children and his wealth.

Job's statement is not to suggest that he didn't become disillusioned, or that he expressed perfect understanding of God's plan and readily accepted what was happening in his life. Nor did he fall to his knees, declaring, "I got a feeling everything is going to be alright." In fact, considering this series of ordeals, and God allowing such calamities to befall him at one time, Job began to question the reason for his own birth. After all, Job was human like you and me, and even though he was a perfect, just, and upstanding man, he still drew the conclusion that God was the source behind his troubles.

Job himself stated, in Job Chapter 6, verse 4, "For the arrows of the Almighty are in me; my spirit drinks their poison; the terrors of God are arrayed against me." Job was not shy in expressing his disturbance over his sickness and crediting God for his suffering. This poetic lament clearly reveals his grief-stricken state of mind. Who could blame him? Recall, Job was a man as we would enviously describe as a person who "had it all". No one would blame Job for becoming salty about his dreadful state and (seemingly) sudden fall from grace.

Yet, after lamenting over his troubles, Job drew strength and in the height of his affliction, turned to God instead of using his circumstances to isolate himself from God. Here we find the difference between Job's behavior and typical behavior—when deep in a trial, we too often allow the pressure of the situation to prompt us to transfer blame to God—finding room to dishonor him with language and contemptuous behavior rather than turning to God the way Job did. Even though Job credited God for his troubles, he remained steadfast, unmovable, always summoning faith to place hope in God.

Job's behavior teaches us to never give up hope in God or allow the magnitude of our trials to cause us to distrust Him. We may blame God; however, we must remain fervent in holding on to our faith and believe He is able to turn our situations around. Regardless of how dire our circumstances may appear at any given time, we must maintain our faith.

If we followed Job's lead, perhaps we would find comfort during the most disappointing moments. Although Job felt God was behind his affliction, he did not sell out on God like some of us are prone to do. What I mean by "selling out on God" is questioning God's sovereignty as if we are on his level and He owes us an explanation when we cannot understand or accept His ways. We seem to forget that God is the creator, we are His creation. We "sell out on God" when we insist that God's ways are troubling more than righteous, and if we were Him, we wouldn't run the universe the way He does. We declare that life is unfair and question why God would allow us to suffer if he loves us. We are almost suggesting that we could do a better job if we were on the throne instead of God. Our perspective causes us to grow bold and foolishly irreverent as we ask dishonorable questions. "If God is omniscient, why would He allow us to go through more than we can bear?"

Instead of using acrimonious language in addressing a holy, righteous God, we would be wiser to remember what Job stated. "Though he slay me, I will hope in him." It is foolish for us to think we should understand God and God's ways. In fact, God tried to help us avoid this impudent behavior by explaining to us foolish human beings this one important truth—a truth that if heeded, would stop us from having so much consternation toward Him. In the Book of Isaiah, Chapter 55, verses 8 and 9 we see:

"'For my thoughts are not your thoughts; neither are your ways my ways,' declares the LORD. 'For as the heavens are higher than the earth, so are my ways higher than your ways and my thoughts than your thoughts.'

The word of the LORD as recorded by Isaiah should ring out as a constant reminder to us all that God is not on our level. Rather, He is "high and lifted up," (Isaiah 6:1 ESV).

God does not process information like we do, nor does He behave like us. God does not and cannot condescend to man's inferior, finite intellect. God does not need to process information to formulate thoughts, because He is the origin of the information. Nor do God's ways or methods reside in the same stratosphere as ours. *When man thus believes that he is capable of questioning God, this simply exposes our innate desire to represent God or, more coarsely stated, expose our God complex.*

Recall how Eve and Adam were presented with the notion that disobeying God would lead them to becoming like Him, and so they did. They decided being like God was more important than obeying Him. Being like God was more provocative than being obedient to Him, thus exposing Adam and Eve's inner desire of being equal to the Almighty. I hear what you are saying, "That's not me, I don't desire to be equal with God, so therefore I don't have a God-complex." I respectfully suggest to you that this is not the factor that determines whether or not you have a God complex. Those of us who suffer from this complex share this in common: we demand to know what God is doing, or we must understand why He chose a particular course of action with respect to the outcome of our lives. We sometimes insist on having the privilege of knowing the nature of the outcome, demanding a seat at the table when God is drawing up plans that include us.

I find this quite interesting, that the very people who make these demands of God are some of the very same who suggest to their own children that they don't have a right to question their parents.

Consider this: When man willfully obeys God, man fulfills his role as a servant, thus honoring his responsibility of remaining faithful through obedience. Conversely, when servants boldly approach the throne of God contentiously questioning His ways, they abandon their true position of servanthood and climb independently upon God's throne, unconsciously seeking to dethrone him in their hearts and minds. This ungodly display of wickedness and equal measure of foolishness is what leads to our twisted rationale—justifying our own pitiful reaction to events in life we will never understand with our finite minds. Therefore, trusting God is paramount to living a peaceful, harmonious existence, which preserves and protects mental well-being.

Some of us share the absurd notion that we are within our rights to question God when we don't agree with certain situations, or when we don't understand what God is up to in our lives. I must tell you, I am totally against this premise of the Created having a right to question the Creator. And before you start spouting to justify mortal rights, allow me to present the basis for my reasoning.

For one, I strongly feel that questioning God demands that God must condescend to our level, to hold counsel with us. Let me correct this irrational and irreverent thinking. God does not owe us anything, certainly not an explanation. Job found this out the hard way, when he decided to question God during his time of suffering, only to hear God respond, "Where were you...?" (Job 38:4-7 ESV).

Secondly, this assumption that we are within our boundaries to question God flips the script, declaring that God is our servant and He exists to serve us, therefore He must answer to us, instead of the other way around. I don't expect everyone to agree, but my response to those who disagree with me is simple. Go ahead with your bad self. I find this behavior highly contradictory given the belief that God is sovereign. We dismiss and diminish His sovereignty by insisting He is also subject to inquiry from mere mortals of His own creation. We are not His peers.

Finally, if God is subject to our line of questioning every time we feel like calling Him to the witness stand, this eliminates the core concept of a higher power. Don't allow your need to question God to marginalize your need to trust Him. When we doubt His sovereignty, we challenge His very existence.

Understandably, all do not share the same level of trust in God. Some are still growing in faith. However, once you have placed your faith in

God, it is hard to argue that trust and faith must grow together if we desire to have peace of mind that supports emotional stability in this uncertain world. In fact, the news headlines provide us considerable evidence of people with seemingly successful lifestyles who are emotionally suffering. This proves we cannot rely on riches or material possessions for healthy self-esteem, inner peace, or contentment.

Many of us are guilty of having a divided heart, maintaining our trust in things rather than placing sole and total trust in God. Instead, we continue to operate out of a duplicitous mindset, wondering if God is truly deserving of our unconditional love and trust. Some of this complacency is perpetuated by painful memories we hold God accountable for, resentment we unconsciously nurture against God, for allowing a painful or traumatic situation to occur in the first place. This causes God to become the target of our blame rather than the object of our affection.

I surmise that David and Job shared something in common that allowed them to remain faithful to God during their darkest times. I believe the commonality between these two men was their intimate relationship with God prior to their stormy seasons.

Thus, if their relationship with God kept them from throwing shade (criticizing) God, the contrary may be true about us. Our fragmented or non-existent relationship with God is what allows us to dishonor Him, rationalizing through a screen of unjust contempt and indifference towards Him. As you can see, we have a lot working against us, causing us to transfer blame and behave impudently to the very one that can carry us through our darkest moments and deliver us from whatever strife we are experiencing.

Most parents have dealt with children acting out because they couldn't have their way. They became the recipient of their child's anger since the child perceived their parents were wrong for denying them their request, and because they wanted something the parent could provide if they wanted to, the child was resentful. Sound familiar? This is the same way we treat God. The very persons the child will need again are the ones the petulant child directs their anger towards and turns their backs on, treating them like an enemy. This emotional disillusionment between parent and child is ironically the same warped idealism we serve up to God. Both sets of relationships suffer because the one in authority is blamed for the undue suffering of the child. How do we correct this self-centered, foolish behavior? First, we need to recognize that God is not on our level, and we will never dethrone God no matter how discontented or disconcerted we are. Second, the more we desire to understand God rather than trust Him exposes the God complex we all seem to share, which hinders our ability to keep faith alive.

Finally, until we can trust God, we will consistently have a fragmented and weak relationship with Him. This sets in motion a vicious cycle that renders spiritual growth virtually impossible Proverbs 3:5, 6 starts out by exhorting us to, "Trust in the LORD with all your heart, and do not lean on your own understanding. In all your ways acknowledge Him and He will make straight your paths." Can you say you trust God with and undivided heart, an unpolluted mind and a surrendered life?

Chapter 4

The Envy that is Birthed

Living constantly under the dark shadows of your past prevents living in the moment, and eventually can offset God's plan for your future. Unfortunately, this realization is rarely obvious to the person embattled in struggle. Inevitably, they sink to inexhaustible feelings of resentment towards those who have seemingly walked an easier or more successful path. Before they can adjust, their feelings cultivate a bitter root that produces unjust criticism, judgement, and backbiting. This, my friend, is the evolution of the green-eyed monster's cousin, called envy.

Envy is the wicked first cousin of jealousy. It dogmatically pursues each victim and unsuspecting foe. Where jealousy is content with making strides toward "keeping up with the Joneses," envy wants to undermine the Joneses—covertly or overtly—because of their possessions, status, and wealth. Understandably, jealousy grows out of wanting what someone else has for ourselves. However, if our heart is left unchecked, envy will supersede jealousy and determine, "I want what you have and furthermore, I have decided you do not deserve the things in your possession."

Envy takes scrutiny of other lives to an entirely different level, as unprovoked, unwarranted judgment. Deep down, I hope we all know that desiring something only because someone else has it is just sad.

Consequently, when we allow our heads to roam in this situation, we allow our corrupted thoughts to poison our hearts towards others without provocation. We lower ourselves to hating on someone because of their possessions, indiscriminately exposing a side of our character that should shame us before man, and definitely before God.

The sad truth is this untamed envy stems from our attitude towards God based on our struggle with our own successes and failures. Our self-examination and constant comparison of our lives with the lives of others, has led us to a place of discontentment, self-doubt, bitterness, and yes, envy. Self-evaluation was never meant to cause dysfunction, yet when coupled with constantly comparing one's life to another, mental chaos ultimately ensues. This has reached a crisis of epic proportions in our current society that largely centers on and around social media, where comparison to others has taken on unprecedented implications.

Because this cycle of behavior is powerfully habitual, envy is always lurking just a few steps away waiting for a chance to pounce and trigger a reaction of feeling disenfranchised by God and others. Therefore, I find it necessary to expose the behavioral pattern that develops when we turn self-examination into self-criticism. Beware of this, since the muscles of criticism have now developed, and rarely are they wasted only on ourselves. This explains why self-haters have such an easy time hating on others—unheralded envy.

30 As soon as Isaac had finished blessing Jacob, when Jacob had scarcely gone out from the presence of Isaac his father, Esau his brother came in from his hunting.

31 He also prepared delicious food and brought it to his father. And he said to his father, "Let my father arise and eat of his son's game, that you may bless me."

32 His father Isaac said to him, "Who are you?" He answered, "I am your son, your firstborn, Esau."

33 Then Isaac trembled very violently and said, "Who was it then that hunted game and brought it to me, and I ate it all before you came, and I have blessed him? Yes, and he shall be blessed."

34 As soon as Esau heard the words of his father, he cried out with an exceedingly great and bitter cry and said to his father, "Bless me, even me also, O my father!"

35 But he said, "Your brother came deceitfully, and he has taken away your blessing."

36 Esau said, "Is he not rightly named Jacob? For he has cheated me these two times. He took away my birthright, and behold, now he has taken away my blessing." Then he said, "Have you not reserved a blessing for me?"

Genesis 27:30-36 ESV

I admit that this story of two brothers—who were very different in nature—was never meant to explain the birth of envy in the heart of a man, but we can allow the evidence to paint a picture of what occurs when one child ascertains their sibling has received a unique blessing they were unable to receive themselves. The problem ensues when one child comes to realize the father's blessing was provided individually, not universally; and the growth of an envious spirit is born.

Follow the narrative carefully; the blessing was decided by the father. The timing of the blessing was decided by the father. The recipient was decided by the father. And finally, the occasion of how the blessing would be delivered was decided by the father. Did you follow the trail of these independent and autonomous sequence of events?

Clearly, the one receiving the blessing was not involved in the decision-making process. In fact, they had no control over their father's thoughts or actions. Benevolence should never stir up envy towards the recipient because the situation is out of their control. This is not to say we have a right to call out the one granting the blessing, either, because they have a right to their choices. Instead, we must fall in line and wait patiently, with pregnant expectations of our own window opening in heaven.

One important fact to acknowledge which will reduce or eliminate the stronghold envy and jealousy can hold over the mind, is that God's business is just that, God's business. Do yourself a favor and mind your business while acknowledging that God is God all by Himself, and He does not need you to review His criteria for blessing others. Furthermore, He does not require your permission, nor do you have a seat on the Board of Directors in Heaven for approving and co-signing God's choices.

The second important fact you must embrace, is that all blessings are not meant to have universal disbursement. Although the father in the story clearly meant to bless the eldest son, when he found out he was taken advantage of by the youngest son, he didn't reverse the disbursement. Therefore, if you swiftly resolve in your mind and heart that God does not have to operate according to equal opportunity guidelines, jealousy and envy will cease from controlling your emotions. Trust me when I tell you, freedom is knowing blessings need not be universal, and the benevolence of God belongs only to God. Freedom!

I realize shaking off the chains of jealousy and envy can prove difficult, often depending on the number of years one has been shackled to these controlling deceivers. Therefore, gaining freedom requires a dedicated strategy. I offer to you one option that will require you to develop trust and avoid self-reliance. This single, powerful change requires turning your past over to God.

Don't become discouraged, this is not as difficult as it sounds. Let me assure you that you can do this by renewing your mind. That's correct, you read that right. Failing to accomplish this one action in life will prove an emotional barrier that will continually trip you up and prevent spiritual growth. Therefore, your starting point is not a mind bender, but a journey to permanent emotional freedom, the renewing of your mind.

Feeling envy towards those we believe are more successful than we can cause us to disconnect our lives from the God we praise for saving us. God obviously gave them more advantages in life than He gave us, hence the reason for their success and our lack of it. God did us a disservice because he did not provide us the same opportunities or intellectual capacity that He gave to others. Thinking God set us up for a setback is exactly the reason why the Bible warns us against this mindset: "But if you have bitter jealousy and selfish ambition in your hearts, do not boast and be false to the truth. This is not wisdom that comes down from above, but is earthly, unspiritual, demonic. For where jealously and selfish ambition exist, there will be disorder and every vile practice." (James 3:14-16 ESV)

These two verses expose the truth. The problem is not with others, or God, the problem stems from a misguided heart. A heart governed and guided by an over-zealous desire to achieve, feeds the bitter root of jealousy towards those who have seemingly 'arrived'. Furthermore, these verses explain the disorderly conduct associated with this unspiritual thinking, which only drives us toward more extreme and ungodly behaviors.

Toxic attitude and beliefs often cause debilitating setbacks because you have kept yourself from putting forth the effort required to succeed in life. There is no wonder why the Bible tells us, "A heart at peace gives life to the body, but envy rots the bones." (Proverbs 14:30 NIV) Pay attention, please, God is not blocking your path to success. You have ultimately erected roadblocks in your own path to achievement. Until you change your thought process, you will continually hinder your belief that you can do better, which diminishes your willingness to try harder, all while continuing to envy the success of others. This behavior consistently triggers thoughts of inadequacy, feelings of mediocrity, and the cycle of failure goes on.

How do these dangerous patterns start? Are you curious? These unfruitful thoughts typically arise when we are laser-focused on ourselves; when all we see, think about, and discuss is ourselves. Spending such an exorbitant amount of time focused inward causes a person to become self-absorbed and self-centered. Consequently, moving in and out of disparaging thoughts creates a feeling of being trapped with no way out. You see your life as a no-win situation. Subsequently, any temporary setback becomes a reason to fall into a state of depression, a lonely and dark place, fueling resentment towards yourself and God.

Let me ask you, how is your relationship with God? Do you feel close, or do you feel far from Him? Do you sometimes doubt His love for you, even while believing Christ died for you because of God's universal love for all humanity?

If you don't feel close to our Heavenly Father and sometimes doubt His love for you, consider that He sacrificed His only son so we can have a relationship with Him; then I hope you can see the need for renewing your mind.

We cannot live like God is our enemy when He gave His son, Jesus Christ to eliminate the enmity between Himself and man. The Bible expressly teaches, "For He Himself is our peace, who has made us both one and broken down in His flesh the dividing wall of hostility (Ephesians 2:14 ESV). We are also taught, "For if, while we were God's enemies, we were reconciled to Him through the death of his son, how much more, having been reconciled, shall we be saved through his life" (Romans 5:10 NIV). Brothers and sisters, God has sacrificed His son to secure our salvation and make peace with us. The time has come for us to stop allowing our envy to stir up feelings of false and foolish enmity between us and God.

Jesus Christ was God's one-man wrecking crew, tearing down the wall of hostility our sins built, and now we have the audacity to allow our own thoughts of envy, feelings of inadequacy rebuild that wall, brick by brick? Can you see the deceptive nature of thoughts dictating our behavior and driving a wedge between us and our loving Father? Truly, we must change the way we perceive God's hand in our lives. The answer is not to feel disenfranchised by Him when we can't find our way through unsettling experiences.

Where have I seen this before? Oh yeah, the children of Israel. When God delivered them from under the hard, tyrannical rule of the Pharaoh, three times they cursed their freedom while facing uncertain situations. When they reached the Red Sea with Pharaoh in hot pursuit, they cried out in fear, "Is it because there are no graves in Egypt that you have taken us away to die in the wilderness? What have you done to us in bringing us out of Egypt? Is not this what we said to you in Egypt: Leave us alone that we may serve the Egyptians? For it would have been better for us to serve the Egyptians than to die in the wilderness." (Exodus 14:11-12 ESV)

The people who previously called on the Lord for deliverance from Egyptian rule were the same people faulting God because they were facing an apparent no-win situation, experiencing extreme discomfort compounded with an unknown future ahead of them. Why did they complain after God had previously displayed his faithfulness through deliverance? Simple, because they allowed fear to overrule their faith in God, blinding them of their historical relationship with Him. Notice how they imagined dreadful conclusions in their minds which dictated the level of fear in their hearts. *Beware of allowing fear to foil your faith.*

"Would that we had died by the hand of the Lord in the land of Egypt, when we sat by the meat pots and ate bread to the full, for you brought us out into the wilderness to kill this whole assembly with hunger." (Exodus 16:3 ESV)

God didn't change, yet their faith failed when they were challenged with a different dilemma than the day before. At least three times after God delivered them from Egypt and showed Himself capable of taking care of His children, they enabled setbacks in their faith. Have you also allowed negative experiences to cause you to desert your faith and forget your history with God? Shameful, that we act just like the children of Israel when we start to feel our backs are against the wall and do not see a way out. When will we learn to allow God's faithfulness to stomp louder down the corridors of our minds and our fears? Thank God his faithfulness towards us is independent of our faith in him. What happens when we fail to grow and live with a renewed mind?

Chapter 5

Problems Associated with Old Habits

Some individuals never see the error of their ways—unable or unwilling to make the necessary adjustments in their lives to obey the law. Instead, they attempt to perfect their felonious behavior, add to their rap sheet, and eventually become career criminals. They expend their energy thinking of ways to improve their street smarts to avoid being caught, rather than using their time to learn a lawful skill or meaningful trade. Rather than change their mind about how they view their life of crime, they design ways to beat the system, paving the way to being repeat offenders and losing their freedom once again. Only a change of mind would result in behavior changes that might alter their lifestyle.

There is a scripture that could serve them well which tells us the advantage of living with a renewed mind. This passage provides evidence that we can improve emotional stability and quality of life by refining the way we think. However, if we fail to renew our minds, then negative thinking floods our perspective and will invariably burden and cripple us with uncertain and false data. The scripture I am referring to states:

"Finally, brothers, whatever is true, whatever is honorable, whatever is just, whatever is pure, whatever is lovely, whatever is commendable, if there is any

excellence, if there is anything worthy of praise, think about these things."
Philippians 4:8 ESV

If you pay careful attention to the language of the text above, each adjective the writer employs is worth thinking about. They each and collectively have positive connotations. Making a habit of thinking this way can prevent unhealthy, troubling thoughts and instead foster a healthy emotional atmosphere for improved mental well-being. It is essential to put forth effort toward achieving positive thoughts—to keep our minds fresh, strong, and free—allowing us to live forward.

The danger in not moving forward, and instead allowing negative thoughts to rule your mind, is that you begin to believe negative ideas about yourself and your life, which can too easily become a self-fulfilling prophecy. In short, when we allow—and indeed, enable—negative energy to consume us, it creates a toxic living environment, and our personal wellness is corrupted.

The damage of negative thoughts does not occur in one event. It grows pervasive over time, subtly sneaking into many aspects of life. We repeat negative words that create a cycle and safe place for negative thoughts. Before long, the mind starts to believe its own poison. You may shrink from opportunities that others step up for on a regular basis, thinking to yourself:

"What's the use of trying? nobody will hire me anyway."

"I am not going to waste my time trying again. It never works out for me."

"I give up, this is embarrassing."

Notice how these words start to dictate their actions and those actions precipitate the reality they themselves created. When we don't believe we can succeed, we avoid challenges others readily face.

You may find yourself skipping and avoiding social engagements, because you aren't proud of how things are going for you. You don't want anyone to ask, "how's it going?" because you don't have an exciting or positive answer. You may find yourself lacking energy, skipping exercise, eating a poor diet. It all starts to spiral and you feel out of control, like you may never get back on track.

I have good news, dear readers. The problems we all face at times do not have to be as severe or as permanent and damaging as we perceive them to be in the moment. The issue is not reality as we see it, but instead the downtrodden reality driven by negative thinking, which ultimately leads to no more effort or hope for a better outcome. Without hope or effort, people too often find themselves trapped in a self-created cycle of destruction. I am here to tell you, it does not have to be this way, if only minds remain open to positive thoughts.

I am glad Thomas Edison didn't allow dark thoughts to preclude him from continuing to pursue an electric source of light. Historians tell us he failed countless times before he succeeded. Regardless of how many times he felt defeated and frustrated, he did not give up. He did not allow his multiple setbacks to allow negative thoughts to creep in and fester. He didn't let incremental failures demotivate or discourage him from trying again and again.

This stands to reason why the Apostle Paul urged the Philippian Church to avoid being governed by negative thoughts and rather develop a mindset of more positive thinking. Interesting how the first thought pattern he instructed them to focus on was "whatever is true". He did not tell them to focus on what they felt was true, or what they through was true, nor the perception of truth. Instead, he told them to think on actual truth. Why? Because perceived truth can and eventually will become an imaginary reality.

Throughout history, wars have erupted based on perceived wrongdoing; brothers have fought and sometimes harmed their own brothers over false data; sisters have fought and, in some cases, harmed their own sisters due to a misunderstanding. Why? Because of a perceived reality that festered in someone's mind long enough to become their own false truth. Educated people have walked away from well-paying jobs, simply because they perceived a promotion was more valuable than a steady paycheck. Some people were certain God told them to quit their jobs and they ultimately lost their homes, resultant to what they thought was truth. Tell me, which thought was true?

The warning is this: we all have the innate ability to create our own truth, sometimes to the detriment of ourselves, our families, and even our friendships. The indisputable truth is we have no one to blame for causing this damage except ourselves. Clearly, we can agree that we need to guard our thoughts until we learn to refuse negative thinking. If you study the list of phrases Paul suggested, you will discover none that are emotionally disturbing or harmful mentally. On the contrary. The terms are perfectly refreshing and mentally soothing from a collective sensibility for us all.

Even if you disagree with Paul's list, of course each of us must determine which thoughts are worth ruminating on. My only point here is it's doubtful you will find something negative in his words, and the perspective I desire to leave with you is that your thoughts have a way of governing your outlook on life, affecting not only the way you think, but also how you feel and potentially live. If left unguarded, thoughts become a pattern that define who you are. This is a risk we must be mindful of and avoid. For example, most negative people are oblivious to the fact they criticize frequently, complain constantly, or suffer from the propensity to practice self-deprecating behavior. It becomes toxic for the individual, and for everyone around them.

Unfortunately, these insidious, habitual practices become personality traits the practitioners begin to ignore and uncharacteristically embrace. This is why most people who struggle with these behaviors become resentful and defensive when confronted and asked to change, even when confronted by friends and loved ones simply trying to disclose their unwelcomed practices. Defensive responses are understandable, given that the perpetrators feel their very personalities are under attack.

This explains the difficulty many have with breaking free to develop a more positive outlook on life, even after giving our lives to Christ. When he told us to renew our minds, Paul provided a way to jumpstart the process of breaking free from mental and emotional bondage that can delay spiritual growth. I believe something we rarely consider is how much our emotional and mental state plays a part in our spiritual development as Christians. No wonder the Bible plainly addresses our minds throughout scripture, signaling the need for operating with a sound mindset as we pursue the mind of Christ. As if to say, the battle we face as Christians is two-fold: spiritual and mental.

The battle looks something like this, professing Christ as your LORD and Savior, yet still questioning God's love for you based on life's experiences. Additionally, believing Christ died for your sins, freeing you from the bondage of sin; yet never experiencing the joy and freedom Christ provides for those He saved because of lingering mental bondage. Most troubling, is never focusing on the magnitude of grace afforded to you through the suffering and death of Christ, because your thoughts are locked and self-centered. Subsequently, you feel alone and emotionally weak, even though, *"He who is in you is greater than he who is in the world."* (1 John 4:4 ESV)

Unfortunately, fighting on the battlefield for our LORD with this emotional baggage causes us to fight the good fight as a wounded soldier—in full armor, but never feeling fit for battle. These feelings exist not because of any truth. On the contrary, Christians are well equipped for battle: "Belt of truth, breastplate of righteousness, shoes of readiness, shield of faith, and the helmet of salvation" is the wardrobe all Christians have in their spiritual closets. (Ephesians 6:11-20 ESV). However, if we never renew our minds we cannot suit up for battle.

Although we are privileged benefactors of complete freedom, granted through Christ's battle on the cross, we still permit ourselves to live in mental bondage that prevents us from living life victoriously as children of God. We forfeit joy provided to us by our loving Lord and Savior simply because we are overwhelmed by our daily emotional struggles, worries over feeling accepted or rejected by our fellow man, all while professing acceptance by God the Father into his glorious family afforded by the blood of Christ.

Are you following the trail of deception that remains alive and well in our minds and keeps us at an emotional distance, even though we are brought near to God by the finished work of Christ? Can you see the difficulty of living the Christian life this way, never quite able to "approach the throne of grace" (Hebrews 4:16 ESV)? All because we have feelings that perhaps we do not deserve grace, or worse, we question whether we have received the grace of God in the first place.

A person living with an un-renewed mind remains an active pawn on the enemy's board game, aiding the opponent in winning the battle against them from the inside. My Christian friends, this should not remain a constant theme in our lives. *God never intended for Christians to live in emotional bondage while being spiritually free.* This inner turmoil will only cause a child of God to resemble a person struggling with some form of mania, living on an emotional roller coaster ride—riding the highs of Sundays and experiencing lows throughout the rest of the week.

If we are not careful, despite having easy access to joy, we can manage to live a joyless existence, day after day. If we are not mindful, we can have the peace of God, yet live without experiencing inner peace. We must always guard against being used by the enemy to disturb the peace; rather than being used by the Father to operate as a peacemaker.

Can you see how living this way causes our faith to appear disingenuous as we claim to love and serve the true and the living God, yet appear not to embody His peace? *God saved us by the atoning death of His Son, granting us peace with him by appeasing his wrath towards us.* "Therefore, since we have been justified by faith, we have peace with God through our LORD Jesus Christ" (Romans 5:1 ESV).

Hence, we must fight for the right to live with a renewed mind, to live free, fruitful, and productive lives unencumbered by past mistakes, sins, and transgressions; where we no longer face penalties for our misdeeds. Lord, that's peace!

As Christians, we have blood-bought rights, rights that we should stake claim to and live out for the rest of our existence in freedom. *Shameful for us to profess the suffering of Christ to the world, only to live as if His suffering was in vain.* Review your life, and if you are living the Christian life without a renewed mind, then make every effort to "forget what is behind" and "walk in newness of life" (Romans 6:4 ESV).

This is by the way, the right of every believer in the finished work of Jesus Christs, to live at peace. Do not forfeit your rights

Facts Promote Pain: Embrace Forgiveness

Eventually, we must learn to realize that living with emotional idols has a detrimental effect on us all. This behavior resurrects painful experiences as long as we continue to revisit the ordeals of our past. Unfortunately, judging by our actions, attitudes, and conversations, not many of us received this memo, or we did and refused to read it.

I must admit that I too was once guilty of ruminating on the past. My behavior was fueled by unforgiveness. Hold up, wait a minute. Can lack of forgiveness cause inability to leave painful experiences alone and move on with life? My answer: *absolutely*.

First, allow me to briefly describe my experience with a painful memory that I refused to let fade away. For years, I refused to forgive my own dear mother for a mistake she made when I was a young child. Today, I call this incident a mistake on her part, but years ago I regarded it as a betrayal toward her one and only son. The short story is my mom took someone else's word over mine.

Based on her examination of the facts as she reviewed them, she punished me for something I was not guilty of, because of something someone else told her. However, shortly after punishing me, someone came to my defense and provided her with the real story. Unfortunately, the damage was already done, and for years I would bring up this story, trying to rub her mistake in her face. I am not proud of this. It was an unadulterated lack of forgiveness on my part, showing long-term blame and shame to the one who birthed me, cared for me, loved on me, and supported me unconditionally over the years.

An unforgiving heart prevented me from shaking the memory of feeling betrayed, and in return, I betrayed her with my attitude towards her. Years later, during a conversation with my mom, my old unforgiving heart started bursting through and I brought up that old story again. This time, something happened. As I was reminding her of her mistake, I finally saw the pain I was causing her by the expression on her face. Instead of feeling pleased with my efforts, my cold heart began to break, this time from my own cruel mistake and shame.

That day, I discovered that unforgiveness was not something I desired to carry around in my heart. I had witnessed up close how unforgiving behavior could drive a wedge between me and the people I loved. By hurting my mom, I was inflicting pain on myself. Pay careful attention to my words. Lack of forgiveness is a large part of why there is so much pain in families and friendships. We sometimes think we are hurting others, those who have hurt us, but that results in lack of forgiveness for ourselves when we make significant mistakes, and unforgiveness towards God (since we are guilty of blaming Him for our past), even though God is blameless.

When we learn to forgive, we experience relief and freedom. Forgiveness allows us to release the pain we carry around in our hearts, which is void of any benefit to us. The only reward for living with resentment and bitterness is lasting emotional suffering. This is something I have personally experienced and learned the hard way.

The day I witnessed the pain on my mother's face was the day I felt the effects of unforgiveness; selfishly driven by the need to avenge my own pain and disappointment. Pain I first felt years ago, yet pain I kept alive simply because I never heard the words: "I was wrong", "Please forgive me". I felt compelled to force my mother to own up to the fact she made a mistake and hurt me as a child. The man felt the need to avenge the pain the child experienced, only because the man continued to carry the pain around from childhood.

People, do yourselves and others a favor. Abort the need to seek revenge; rush to forgive instead. And if you need some additional motivation because you believe the person does not deserve to be released from blame and shame, then read the words of Jesus: *"If you do not forgive others their sins, my heavenly father will not forgive you of your sin." (Matthew 6:15)* Help us, Lord!

Keep this one fact in mind, when you forgive someone that you believe wronged you, you don't only release them, you also release yourself. Do not wait for someone to apologize. Just forgive them. Do not wait for someone to express to you that they were wrong. Just forgive them. Stop holding yourself hostage to the mistakes of others. Stop carrying the unnecessary burden of a grudge you refuse to release because of someone else's transgression. Lose that unwanted extra weight and exercise God's weight loss plan called forgiveness.

Yes, the fact is others have caused us pain by delivering unkind words, acting intentionally rude and unloving, or even being thoughtless towards us. These are just the facts. What is also a fact is we cannot erase the pain of our past. However, we can use our pain to benefit others. Allow me to illustrate this with a story. While in the third grade, my oldest child came home from school one day, experiencing pain in her abdomen. After asking her a few questions, I called her pediatrician to help me decide how to best help her feel better.

From our discussion, the doctor stated that if she didn't feel better and I wanted to take her to the hospital, to take her to the children's hospital in Jacksonville. Normally, when children experience stomach pain, we treat the symptom and give them something to settle their stomach, because we assume the pain stems from something they ate. I didn't do that with my daughter, instead I examined her stomach and pressed on the area where her appendix was located and released my hand quickly to see her reaction. Her reaction helped me decide she needed immediate medical attention. Why did I feel her stomach this way? Because of my own history with an appendicitis attack when I was only a few years older than she was at the time. I will never forget the trauma I went through or how my doctor examined my stomach to determine that I needed immediate medical attention. My painful past with spending months in the hospital, fighting for my life was not just a part of my history. When it mattered the most, I used my traumatic experience to help my child during a critical time in her own life.

Once the medical staff examined her later that night, they discovered she had a rather large urachal cyst that was putting pressure on her bladder, causing her immense pain. I might have waited to take her to the doctor the next morning, or attempted to treat her symptoms and waited to see if she would eventually feel better, but that would have only made matters worse. My past painful experience and emergency appendectomy as a child prompted my decisive action to take her to the emergency room. That unpleasant history allowed me to help ease the pain of someone I care for deeply.

I am trying to express as clearly as I can how our pain can serve to help relieve somebody else's pain if we don't become too consumed with ourselves. We can start by not allowing hurtful trauma to make our lives miserable by recalling every low point or deep valley experience. We never know when the awful experience we previously faced can aide someone else's journey. Don't waste your pain!

The Morning Ritual: Be Careful of How You Jumpstart Your Day

'Morning blues' are perpetuated by dreadful thoughts that hit us like an emotional hangover, often precipitated by some lingering memory of an unsettling experience. When this occurs, our mornings are invaded by toxic thoughts that become our 'morning wake-up ritual,' exercised within our minds as we start each day. The sad truth is this destructive ritual presumes that today will start where yesterday ended. The boss will lean into you, working on your nerves like they did yesterday. The thought of having to deal with the disturbing behavior of that same co-worker who challenges you emotionally, day after day; the child, the spouse, the neighbor, the car, the bills... Some disturbing thoughts that make us feel trapped provoke a not-so-cheerful morning greeting when the day has just begun.

Here you are, waking up to the gift of a new day, only to succumb to the presence of a toxic thought which steals your newly delivered, undeserved gift and casts a shadow on the dawn of a new morning. What a way to start the day! Oh, but wait! Worse than having these negative thoughts is the compelling need to discuss out loud with yourself or anyone you can disturb who will listen. That last sentence might sound a little harsh, but this behavior is disturbing to both the sufferer and the people enlisted to hear your perpetual venting.

All of us make a conscious decision when we experience difficult times. We can try hard to adjust and adapt the best way we know how, or we can allow difficult experiences to overwhelm us with feelings of how unfair life is, leaving us with only bitterness. Make no mistake, it is a choice.

Drawing the conclusion that life is unfair only serves to deepen emotional scars and toxic resentment. This perspective becomes self-inflicting punishment that does not relieve one's burdens or boost self-esteem. Instead, this increases heaviness on hearts, minds, and souls. Too many conclude that God has withheld something, or they have missed out on some blessing in life, when God has given us the best blessing of all, His son, Jesus Christ.

Mornings should bring thoughts of new possibilities, opportunities to rebuild and restore hope for new chances and better choices. We start each morning by saying, "good morning," because there is hope the day ahead will indeed produce something good; some new and exciting experience that may usher in a better day than before. We cannot allow infectious thoughts to suffocate hope for a new beginning. Hope is essential for a chance to reset and reboot our yesterdays, to start the day afresh.

Look to this scripture for some encouragement: "Weeping may tarry for the night, but joy comes with the morning" (Psalm 30:5 ESV). This verse is meant to reassure us that sorrow can, does, and will transition out of our lives eventually, and we should live life with hope that brighter days will shine through for us all. Make a conscious effort to avoid blocking your own joy from shining through with the dawn of each new morning. No matter how recently you may have experienced sorrow, never use time as an excuse to wallow in self-pity.

"I just experienced that betrayal last year."

"It was only six months ago when they walked out."

"I saw them yesterday and a flood of emotions rushed over me."

I understand! But notice, the verse above does not dispel the fact that we will experience times of sorrow, nor does it suggest that time is a variable which dictates or delays the arrival of joy in the morning. We all have sorrows, and some of us have experienced hardship more traumatic or more recently than others. What I like is that this scripture does not place a timeline on when we should expect sorrow to fade and joy to enter our lives, despite our woes. Therefore, the arrival of joy is not predicated on the level of sorrow, which suggests that joy could come sooner than later.

Now, I think we all understand that the dawning of a new day does not automatically introduce joy. However, our sorrows don't have to last a lifetime, and therefore we can live with hopeful expectations that joy is on the way. Because as Christians we have the promise of joy living inside of us once the Holy Spirit takes up residence in our hearts. Since that is a spiritual fact, are you delaying your right to experience joyful mornings by obsessively mourning over your yesterdays? Has your mourning ritual eclipsed your morning joy?

In May of 2019, I was booked on a redeye flight from Los Angeles, California to Jacksonville, Florida. When I left Los Angeles that Sunday morning, the initial leg of my flight was on time and my connection in Atlanta, Georgia was showing an on-time departure as well. My goal was to arrive in time to attend a 10:45am ceremony for graduating high school seniors at my church. This was going to be a special service because my son was one of the graduates being honored that morning, and to make the ceremony even more special, he was receiving a scholarship from our church.

All was looking good as we landed in Atlanta. I stepped off the plane to check the departing flights, and the joy of my morning booked its own flight and flew away. Inclement weather in the northeast had disrupted air travel throughout the country and derailed my chances of making the ceremony in Jacksonville on time. I was very upset with the whole situation and did everything I could to catch the earliest flight out of Atlanta to make the service. The best I could do was receive a standby booking on the next departure, and hope and pray for the best. My chances were rather grim since my name was 30-something on the list. It seemed no matter what, I was going to arrive too late to make the service.

Growing more frustrated with each passing moment, I was hungry and angry. But no matter how emotional I became, my emotionalism was not going to change or improve my unfortunate situation. I was stuck in Atlanta until the next flight out and I was going to miss the ceremony, for sure. So, I shifted my focus to the only situation I could fix, my hunger attack, and eventually found something worth eating.

As I was eating at one of the counters in the food court, a young lady in her early twenties sat down next to me and we struck up a conversation. She was rather upbeat and lively for that time of morning, and although I was in no mood for small talk, I did wonder why she was so happy and effervescent. After a brief introduction, I explained my situation to her and then she told me her story. To my surprise, her behavior was the direct opposite of what I would have expected from someone going through her ordeal. You see, the same weather that contributed to the cancellation of my flight out of Atlanta had caused her to become stranded overnight in the Atlanta airport. She explained to me that she had spent most of her day in the airport and slept overnight on a bench while awaiting the next flight to her destination sometime later Sunday morning. Mind you, she was full of joy, and I was sulking and sad, steaming because I was being held at bay for a few additional hours, lamenting over my disappointing turn of events.

I have to confess, after hearing her sad tale yet seeing how she was taking it all in stride, I had to ask why she was not acting miserable like me. She explained since there was nothing she could do to change the situation, there was no need for her to act out or feel down, so she simply chose to face it with joy. I thought to myself, *you sound like a Christian to me.* I thanked her for the conversation because she helped me dial back my emotions, recover my joy, and attempt to ride out the situation since there was nothing I could do to reverse my circumstances.

Honestly, it took effort. I only reluctantly allowed my joy to return. Why? Because I was disappointed and upset, immersed in my feelings. I believed I had a right to feel miserable. After all, why was this bad situation happening to me? I didn't deserve this bad luck. I didn't deserve to miss out on sharing in my son's special moment. Life had sucker punched me and I couldn't fight back. It was difficult to contain my exasperation. Yet, I had a choice to make.

There is a lesson in this for us all. While dealing with situations we can't change, we have a choice to make: we can handle it with joy, or we can sulk and be sad. Never mind whether we deserved the setback. The decision is ours.

So, I decided that morning, if this young lady could let her joy shine through, then so could I. This was a discovery for me, that operating in joy was a conscious choice I had a right to make, since I already had joy residing in my heart. Therefore, I was not going to spend the rest of the morning sulking in silence and acting as if my God wasn't good, simply because of this miserable moment I was experiencing.

As much as I was lamenting over my own personal trouble that morning, I came face to face with the ultimate truth in a trial. As bad as your situation is, there is always someone going through something worse, so thank God your situation is not as bad as it could be.

Do yourself a favor, stop the mourning ritual and let joy arrive. Let the joy of the Lord flow freely in your heart by reminding yourself, *my situation could have been a lot worse.* Block the mourning by reciting these words every morning when God provides you the gift of a new day, "This is the day that the LORD has made, let us rejoice and be glad in it" (Psalm 118:24 ESV). Would you agree you deserve to experience joy? Then learn a new habit and fan your joy into a flame.

Instead of performing the usual dragging morning ritual, try allowing the favor of a new day to produce joy in your heart. Seize the moment and express the excitement of simply being alive.

Don't waste your pain!

The Mistakes of your Past are Preventing you from Moving Forward: Let Go and Grow

I have personally listened to a plethora of messages over the years whereby the orator strove to move listeners beyond the valley of despair, the unending seasons of disappointment, and the agony of life associated with defeat and rejection. Although the messages were on point, doubtful if everyone listened, meditated on the message, or made strides to apply the three points which so eloquently painted the path to recovery. Why, you might ask? Well, there are surely several reasons why listeners fail to apply healing messages, and one is that they have made the pain of their past a keepsake for themselves. They made idols of their mistakes.

You cannot grow when you refuse to let go. An infant is weaned from their mother only to receive a bottle, whereby mother and baby can gain more independence while the baby continues to grow. However, if the mother allows the baby's cries to cripple the child's growth into independence, both mother and child remain locked in a co-dependent relationship that can severely hamper and hurt rather than soothe the child's development. People become so dependent on their past, they refuse to let go regardless of how beneficial the dissociation would be if they did. Somewhere along the way, their painful past has become a pacifier they reach for during low moments rather than something they use as a springboard to brighter days and better tomorrows.

Follow these words carefully, "What you meant for evil, God meant for good." Leave plenty of room for God to work through our adversities. Learn to allow the fruit of your lips to bless Him even while you are still in pain from past mistakes.

The story of Samson in the book of Judges provides us with an illustration of the danger of allowing past mistakes to paralyze the momentum needed to propel forward and eventually reach the destiny of future goals. Those of us who have made significant mistakes can clearly identify the moments and choices that altered our destinies, delaying or even canceling our dreams. Some of us can even recall vividly the details surrounding the events that led to our past failures.

Whether or not you are familiar with the story of Samson and Delilah, I will provide you a brief summary of this memorable biblical story from the Old Testament. Samson was born one of the strongest men in the land for the purpose of avenging God's people against their enemies. Samson, however, had a secret unknown to those who were not very close to him. His secret was the source of his strength. The Bible declares that God endowed Samson with the strength of "ten men": a divine gift given for a divine purpose, for a divinely appointed time.

Upon witnessing this amazing strength, his enemies of course were very curious in discovering the source, hoping to rob him of this mysterious gift and bring him crashing to his knees. Enter Delilah, the antagonist of the story, the enemies' secret weapon—the femme fatale from the pit of hell. She was a woman for hire, paid by Samson's enemies to trick Samson into revealing the source of his unfathomable strength. The rest is history. Samson allowed himself to become worn down by Delilah and reluctantly trusted her with his secret, and true to form, she betrayed his trust and revealed his secret to his enemies.

The source of Samson's strength was derived from his long locks of hair. If a razor never touched his head, Samson's strength remained intact. Once his enemies discovered his secret, they shaved his head, blinded him, and reduced him to a "normal human being", leaving him unable to complete his divinely appointed mission for God. Samson by all intent and purpose was an utter failure, missing the mark without a backup plan to restore his integrity or at least recover some of his dignity. For his failure, he was reduced to being chained to a mill; sentenced to blindly pushing a stone around instead of freely fulfilling his God-given mission, the mission of bringing judgment against the enemies of God.

Sounds familiar, doesn't it? Most of us haven't come close to suffering the fate of Samson or the punishment he endured, yet we feel we can share his failure to pursue and complete his missional assignment before God. We too, have dashed dreams that serve as reminders of what could have been, or guilt from mistakes that caused pivotal diversions, roadblocks that altered the course of our life. Like many of us, Samson allowed pressures in his life to cause him to betray his gift and lose sight of his true goals.

However, unlike most of us, Samson did not allow himself to remain in a defeated state, complaining about his past mistakes to everyone who would listen. Samson did not hang out at the complaint counter of God, asking, "Why did my life turn out this way?" Nor did he play the blame game and incriminate God for not bailing him out. Instead, Samson decided to return to the Lord and call out to Him for help. Samson realized something that few of us ever comprehend, which is that we serve a forgiving and merciful God, a God of second chances.

At the lowest point of his life, rather than berate himself in pity and shame, Samson decided he would instead look up to God for help and redemption. He did not attempt to look inward, only to give up or implode. He did not look around for a friend to sing the blues to. No, at his lowest, saddest, most vulnerable moment, Samson looked to God. I like this about him simply because he did not allow the shame and guilt of his mistakes to rob him of his relationship with God. He turned to the only One that could restore any hope he had for restoration.

Samson did not leave God out of his life at the most crucial moment of his life. He instead sought God, the only true and lasting source of his strength. Samson refused to allow the pains of adversity to drive a wedge between himself and God. Samson did as any child should do when injured by the bullies of life, run to your loving parent who loves and cares for you.

The story of Samson is a remarkable display of how, "all things work together for good" (Romans 8:28 ESV). Notice if you will, the key to that statement was revealed in Samson's story; we must remain in the presence of God, we must never abandon God during times of adversity; we must always seek and trust God, no matter the circumstances.

Because Samson never abandoned God, he was able to fulfill his purpose even when he had fallen short along the way. In God's hands, our failures can still birth our dreams because God is the ultimate visionary that cannot fail. Just because we failed somewhere along the way does not mean we cannot finish if we remain faithful to God. Samson apparently understood one important fact of life: failing isn't final if you find your way back to God before the finale.

Wait a minute, I thought Samson died a horrible death in the end? He did, but he died fulfilling the will of God, and he died on his own terms, not at the hands of his enemies.

Because Samson returned to God, the very mission God sent him to carry out was the last assignment Samson accomplished before he died. And even though his enemies had him blinded and bound, God allowed Samson to avenge his failure by finishing his mission. He destroyed his enemies while they mocked, ridiculed, and laughed Samson to scorn. Samson did not waste his pain.

I agree, the end of Samson's life was unfortunate, but this signals to all of us that our decisions can meet with unfortunate consequences. Therefore, we need to tread carefully and make wise choices that don't lead to ill-fated consequences.

The Ugly Baby Syndrome: Picture Your Life Through the Lens of God

Ugly Baby Syndrome is a terrible practice we infringe upon ourselves as we survey the landscape of our lives. This practice only serves to evoke emotional trauma at the behest of negative behavior and thinking. We speak in narration of our lives in a negative way that suggests there is nothing good, pleasant, worthwhile, meaningful, lovely, or praiseworthy about our existence. We never catch a break, never win, always come up short and end up with the short end of the stick. Everyone else has all the luck, the best of everything, blessed in abundance and loved by God. Everyone except us. Our lives represent that of an "ugly baby".

As we all know, no parent goes around calling their own baby ugly. To a parent, their baby is the most precious child alive; a gift, a blessing, a beauty to behold. Why? Well, because the baby is their child. They love their baby, adore their baby. No matter what the world thinks, their baby is beautiful and their opinion of their child is the only one that matters.

We should take a lesson from this parental perspective when we view and speak of ourselves. Your life is your life, it is the only one you have. Speaking negatively about your life will never serve you in a positive way. Instead, this will cause you to question your existence, and even question God's goodness. Why do you think so many people walk around in states of depression with overwhelming feelings of misery? Could this stem from repeated, overstated, negative opinions of themselves?

Have you ever stopped to evaluate your own negative thoughts and words? Have you assessed the adverse effect your negative viewpoint has on your day-to-day access to joy? Do you see how your attitude colors the way you see your life and relationships?

Take the person who always says that their marriage is a failure or was a mistake. Well, if they always say this then they will always think this, and they will always operate from this vantage point. We do not need a person with a PhD to tell us this negative behavior will eventually erode their relationship and sour their heart for their mate, or vice versa.

Follow me now. A person thinking and speaking this way will start to operate solely based on what they feel and say about their relationship, not because it is necessarily true. Their own behavior will dictate and perpetuate their negative feelings. They will start causing conflict, stirring up strife, looking for sore point buttons to push, and failing to conduct themselves in a way that fosters a loving and fruitful relationship. All because they have already concluded the relationship was not meant to be.

Are you starting to see and sense the destructive element that becomes realized when we feed our minds a toxic diet? Are you starting to see how disastrous negative words are?

Parents always see their own child's beauty, but the truth is some newborn babes do grow into their looks over time. Why is this important? It's simple, your life can transition into a life of joy beyond your wildest dreams. First, stop thinking joy is meant only for the rich and famous or the young and foolish. Joy is meant for those who have accepted Jesus and committed their life to Him. Therefore, regardless of how you view your life today, you can live a life full of joy. Paul encourages the church, the saints of God to "Rejoice in the Lord always; again I will say, rejoice" (Philippians 4:4 ESV).

One of the biggest mistakes we Christians make, regardless of how long we have been saved, is found in this passage of scripture above. We continually try to maintain a connection with happiness when God has provided us with an internal flame called joy. I am not suggesting there is something wrong with happiness, but I will state that if all you have or experience is happiness after being saved, then you may not have as much nor have you experienced as much as you believe.

Happiness is derived from something favorable occurring, whereby we become excited for a time, but then happiness fades when the euphoria dies down. To buy a new car, receive a promotion, or receive a compliment, emotions kick in and we become happy, but only for a short time. Because happiness is tied to an event or situation, it is fleeting and cannot be maintained or restored. However, God provided us with something so much more lasting and amazing, and although also tied to an event (salvation) it is ultimately connected to a person, the Lord Jesus Christ.

The above scripture informs us that our ability to rejoice is made possible through our union with Christ, and Christ alone. Therefore, joy is everlasting and has nothing to do with a change in circumstances or any negative situation. One of the lessons we can learn is that peace is not self-derived, nor is it self-maintained.

The main reason why joy trumps happiness is because, "The joy of the Lord is your strength" (Nehemiah 8:10). As Christians, we are comforted by the fact that our joy and peace are not man-made; therefore, I don't have to search for joy in people, things, or even myself. We have the benefit of having our joy reside in Christ, maintained by Christ and Christ alone. Hence, even if our situations and circumstances never change, we can rest knowing Christ can and will preserve us through our worst experiences.

Paul is reminding the church at Philippi to remember that the source of their joy is Christ, and furthermore, that they have a right—no, a duty—to rejoice, regardless of their current sufferings. This truth is not solely for the Christians at Philippi, but for all of us who are united with Christ through our faith in His finished work on the cross.

So the next time you start to feel down about your life, instead rejoice in the Lord. Your life is not an ugly baby. Heed these words carefully: stop wallowing in self-pity and realize that rain falls in everyone's life, and sometimes the rain causes some flooding. But when the waters start to rise it is not the time to panic, only to prepare to move to higher ground. That time is now. Changing the way you view your life can change the way you live. In the meantime, remember you have a reason to rejoice, you are saved by the blood of Jesus. God gave you the life that you are living; you need to allow this fact to beautify and edify your thoughts, allowing your life to give Him glory. You have a right to rejoice, you are a child of God.

The Feeling of Coming Up Short in Life: Learn to Be Content

Having a sense of contentment allowed the Apostle Paul to avoid the feeling most people develop, that they have somehow come up short in life. This leads to living in self-pity and a lot of complaining. In his book, God Meant it for Good, R. T. Kendall had this to say about self-pity:

"Self-pity jumps to bad conclusions without evidence. It plays into a syndrome of pessimism, feeding itself on the assumption of more bad news. A person like this wants bad news. He does not want to be contradicted. He is so sure things are going to be bad that he almost resents it when one says, 'It may not be that bad.' 'Oh, yes it is, yes, it is,' he answers. The person filled with self-pity is looking forward only to saying, 'I told you so.' "5

Whether we realize it or not, these actions inevitably lead to deep depression and a longing for turning back the hands of time. Unfortunately, this is impossible. This is why learning to become content is such a vital tool for us to employ. Living life with a sense of contentment serves a two-fold purpose for those who choose to embrace this perspective.

First, living with contentment fosters an attitude of gratitude. Instead of feeling as if your life does not measure up, or as if you have not achieved the same level of success as others, contentment helps us to realize we do not even deserve what we currently have. Contentment reminds us that we are not solely responsible for whatever we think we have achieved. Beloved, you will have a difficult time displaying ingratitude when you consider that your life could have turned out worse, and you are most undeserving of the possessions you own or status you have gained.

Secondly, living with contentment produces a spiritual wellness within our souls. You see, one of the synonyms of contentment is serenity. When we live with a sense of contentment, our souls experience serenity, an inner peace that escapes the average person. To have this experience of inner peace demands that we operate in contentment, to walk the bridge that advances our lives to this previously unreachable place.

Unfortunately, some of us never make this journey to contentment, serenity, and inner peace, because we are too focused on trying to prove a right to declare, "I have come up short." This is based entirely on our own evaluation of our lives against the lives of others. The "right" to make this declaration only serves to set us back. What we unconsciously believe is a defense or cushion and shield from reality, is the thing that hinders us from ever reaching the goal.

If you have ever been content at any stage of your life, then you already know the peace this brings. And certainly, you can sympathize with those who forfeit this amazing experience of serene peace and calm.

Chapter 6

Developing New Habits

Finding Contentment: Allow Gratitude to be your Trump Card

Allow me to offer a GPS, to help you find and follow the path of contentment. First, turn the opposite way of self-pity. Self-pity dead-ends at the intersection of "I Have Come Up Short Avenue" and "Depression Lane". Many unfortunate incidents occur daily at this intersection. Avoid this area at all costs. Neither of these roads lead to contentment.

Next, you want to avoid the toll road of comparison. The expense of comparison seems to increase each time travelers make the journey. The toll road of comparison takes from each traveler more than they intended to pay. The sad reality is some people never realize there are other routes to take in life that do not penalize you. But some insist on using the comparison route as if there are no others, eventually stuck with paying the price for their decision. Pay careful attention here: the cost is too great. Avoid this road, whatever you do.

Finally, set your GPS to the town called "Contentment". Obey speed limits as you make your way to this town. The paths are full of traps and rapid, unexpected changes. It isn't always easy to see what's coming round the next bend. Just keep your eyes trained on the road and focus carefully; you should arrive safely to the town of Contentment.

Keep in mind, there is only one main road that leads to this town. It's called, "Play the Hand You Are Dealt". This road is long and becomes narrow at certain points. In some places, it goes from paved to suddenly rocky without notice, but you must keep going. There are seemingly endless detours, but keep going because you will eventually arrive at your destination. Don't become surprised when you see people turning around; you just keep going. Avoid allowing the slow traffic to deter you. Please do not overly concern yourself with distance or delays, or the road construction you encounter—you are on the right track. Believe me, you are heading in the right direction.

One warning: don't believe fake news that the bridge is out. Just keep going. Now, let me give you some sound advice. When you arrive, abide by the rules. But I must warn you, there are no "Pity Parties" allowed. This type of celebration is against the law. In fact, this town prides itself on being the only town that has never held a Pity Party since being founded.

Well, since I am citing a few dos and don'ts, let me tell you about another ordinance—the ordinance against public intoxication. This is not the same as overindulging in alcohol. No, this is being intoxicated with toxic thoughts, leading to toxic discussions, and exhibiting behavior that reveals you have overindulged on toxic thoughts way too long. They will arrest you and throw you in jail. If this is you, I strongly suggest you detox your mind before you arrive.

Those who abide by the rules have such an enjoyable time, they don't want to leave. In fact, no one has left this town of their own volition; however, there have been those that were asked to leave because they refused to abide by the rules. You already know what they did wrong, trying to invite people to pity-parties and public intoxication where they were repeatedly caught vomiting toxic words. Some were even cited for being Peeping Toms because they were caught looking in windows and comparing their lives to others; caught exhibiting the same bad behavior that prevented them from making this journey years ago.

They were all politely asked to leave. Why? Because all these behaviors were against the existing beliefs of the townspeople. Sure, all of them probably dabbled in some of these behaviors in the past. But now that they know better and have repented, they all vowed never to commit these life-altering infractions as long as they live. They detoxed themselves and disassociated themselves from the bad behaviors. Why? Because they, just like the Apostle Paul, could say, "I have learned to be content." They had also discovered the serenity of being content. So, continue to follow the signs, look at your GPS, do yourself a favor and get there.

You may be saying, "That sounds great and all, but I still struggle with moving forward. "I realize abandoning certain behaviors will present a difficult transition, but you first must believe this is possible. Now, I must admit there is something that hinders most of us from making this transition, no matter how much we desire to change the course of our lives.

Avoid Forfeiting Contentment: Don't Live Life with the Glass Half Empty

The best way to avoid forfeiting the right to live in contentment is to guard your perspective on life. Most people I know regard life from one of two perspectives: they either see the glass as half empty, or half full. Can you honestly tell which category you belong to? Your assessment is important for you to successfully live in peace, accepting both sunshine and rain as life unfolds one day at a time.

When we were children, we disliked rainy days with a passion. For you see, our parents forbade us to go outside in the rain. We could not visit our friends, because parents felt we would track mud in our friends' and neighbors' houses if we went door to door in the rain. Thus, the rain became a symbol of disdain until we discovered that mud is a byproduct of rain.

Mud introduced a whole new perspective on rain for us. Once we discovered how much fun it was to play in mud, rain became our best friend. We went from disliking rain to hoping it would come down harder once we saw the slightest drizzle in the sky. What changed for us children? Did the rain change? Did our parents change?

The only change was our perspective once mud pies were discovered. Muddy hands and clothes were discovered. Throwing mud became a new game for us. "Rain, rain go away, come again another day," was no longer a song we cared to sing the way we did before.

The rainy days of life went from being half empty to half full. How do you view your rainy days? If you managed to play with the byproduct that rain brings, then you have begun to see the glass of life as half full. If not, then you struggle in viewing life as half empty. I realize that analogy might not move you, so let us grow up some together, shall we?

I remember transitioning to junior high school and sometimes not feeling like dressing out in physical education class. It seemed like too much trouble on some days, going through all the changing clothes and what not. You had to dress or that was a sure demerit counted against your grade (ain't nobody got time for that), so you dressed out. Well, not on rainy days! On rainy days, sometimes we were cut some slack, especially if the activity was an outside activity. Then we were able to play and do whatever inside activity we choose.

Aw, the beauty of rainy days growing up in junior high. The rain allowed choices during PE. But what about now? For those who have long since moved on from junior high, why should adults view the rain with high value? Because rain is a source of replenishment. Rain refills our reservoirs, lakes and streams, nourishes our grass, and other things. It controls pollen on the worst of days, and once you learn to simply peer out the window at the rain, you can allow it to drift you into a calm place in your mind. What I am trying to articulate is that as we grow up, we all need to allow our perspectives to mature with age and time. This is the sure way to transition from a half-empty to a half-full viewpoint on life.

We have heard the various cliches: 'turning lemons into lemonade,' 'making the best of a bad situation,' 'looking for the silver lining.' Each represents the same positive affirmation, that much of life is all about your attitude and how you perceive situations and circumstances.

Maintaining a Short-Term Memory: Shake Off the Setback

Any good ball player knows that the secret to a successful game, and indeed, a great season, is to operate with a short-term memory. If asked, each good player will tell you this is as important to them as their talent for the sport they play. They would attest to learning early in their careers the healthy habit of leaving the last play or woeful mistake behind them, preventing the memory from interfering with the rest of their game, potentially impacting their season.

There are players who can testify that their inability to escape the lingering memory of missing a big play, heavily affected their performance for the remainder of a game, and in the opinion of some, led to a season-long slump. The potentially game-winning shot taken at the buzzer that bounced wildly off the rim; the would-be winning catch that fell awkwardly through their hands at the end of the game; the final out of the game caused by a strikeout with the go-ahead run stranded on third base.

So, instead of taking a bow to cheers from the crowd for being the clutch player, the heroine or hero were left holding their heads in shame. Instead of euphoria-driven high-fives, they received empty pats on the back as consolation, hearing the dreadful words, "at least you tried," or "better luck next time," infamous words of comfort that never seem to offer much comfort during that long walk of shame back to the locker room.

Honestly, many of us have gone through comparable experiences in our everyday lives, trying hard to succeed and accomplish some goal, only to come up short. The outlook appeared hopeful this time around, only for the outcome to turn out the same. We failed to receive the often-elusive promotion of which we felt so deserving; the relationship that started out so promising, ending again with painful regrets and disappointment; the betrayal of a trusted friend or loved one we put so much faith in, only to have them stab us in the back.

Many of us can confirm that hearing the words "at least you tried," or "better luck next time," never eases the pain or removes the weight of disappointment that sits so heavy on our hearts. When life happens and we are trying to control our emotions, which scene will we allow to unfold? Do we shake off the situation like most good players have learned to do, by keeping only a short memory of our most recent setback, or do we replay and rehash the experience over and over again, keeping the painful emotions alive?

Truly, the choice is ours. Work with me for a moment! Consider the following questions:

- How do you benefit from dwelling on the fact you did not receive the promotion you wanted?
- What are the advantages of ruminating on that failed relationship which ended unexpectedly, causing so much heartache?
- What is there to gain from holding on to the disappointment of betrayal by a trusted friend or loved one?

Can I help you with the answer to all above? Nothing! Nothing! Nothing! Therefore we must develop the skill of keeping a short-term memory. There is nothing positive that results from allowing mistakes to haunt us and control us. Don't waste your pain. If leaving the past behind has always been a struggle for you, then developing the habit of keeping short memories will not come easy or become an immediate reality. However, let's examine the effects of failing to keep a short-term memory of your past. Maybe then you will theorize the benefits once you survey the consequences of choosing to allow your past a quest room in your mind.

Self-Encouragement: Destroy Negative Energy by Looking up to God

If you were to recall difficult periods from your past, you might affirm praying only as a last resort, and admit that praying required a lot of self-encouragement or motivation. Now, I am not referring to those simple, "Help me, Lord!" exclamations. I am referring to those moments when you spend time wrestling with God in prayer, waiting on your change to come. In fact, self-encouragement is the believer's assistant, suggesting the time has come for us to fall on our knees after concluding there is nowhere else to turn.

Have you ever wondered why reaching up for deliverance is more difficult than continuing aimlessly in your struggle? Simply because your own negative energy has wreaked havoc on your self-encouraging will; the inner drive that motivates you to push through pain and keep moving forward. That is why for some of us, prayer is the last resort, not our first line of defense. "Do the opposite: be quick to pray. Stop talking to yourself. Talk to Christ."[6]

Praying cosigns your faith, which affirms your trust and supports your belief system that God can still do the impossible—even when a positive outcome appears improbable—He can work miracles in the midst of misery, and "...is able to do far more abundantly than all we ask or think..." (Ephesians 3:20 ESV).

So, when we revert to dwelling on our past and stirring up negative questions of ourselves—such as, "Why are the people who hurt me excelling in life when I am not?"—we expose the reality that our own negative energy has destroyed our self-encouraging prowess and defeated us from the inside out. Something indeed must change! Would you agree?

As difficult as change is for most of us, once we admit we need to make a change, the next step is to start. Step one is to generate a desire to move forward instead of falling backwards and landing on those same sorry excuses. Step two is to foster a mindset of self-encouragement; something many have discovered when their backs were against the wall. Why? Because "self-motivation is the 'turbocharger' of life."[7] For example, one day, king David, one of the heroes of scripture in the Old Testament, found himself in a most precarious position in his life after being rejected, dejected, and subjected to possible death by his own men.

As the story unfolds in 1 Samuel 29 and 30, David and six hundred of his men joined forces with Achish, King of Gath, several years before the events of our account. Although faithful to the king, the Philistine commanders were all too familiar with David and strongly against trusting him in battle. So, they convinced the king to dismiss David and his men and send them packing to go back home. Unfortunately, their dismissal from the army was the least of their troubles.

We are told in 1 Samuel 30:1-6, that after a three-day journey, David and his men reached their destination only to make a very unsettling discovery. A familiar enemy, the Amalekites, had raided their homes, burned their town, and kidnapped their families. In fact, scripture declares, "Then David and the people who were with him raised their voices and wept until they had no more strength to weep." Life progressed from bad to worse for one of God's servants, although David is lauded in scripture as being, "A man after His own heart..." (1 Sam 13:14).

Both David and his men found themselves in a dark and lonely place in life. In time, his own men sought to soothe their pain by betraying the one in charge, David himself. This was greatly distressing, for the people spoke of stoning him, because all the people were bitter in soul, each for his sons and daughters (1 Sam 30:6).

Wait a minute! Are you seeing this avalanche of troubling events unfold before our very eyes? This is enough to make the strongest of men have an emotional breakdown or reject and turn their backs on God. All this mental overload occurred within a three-day span. Very likely most of us would have rebelled against God for being dismissed by the king. Certainly, finding our families taken captive and the insult of a burned town would stir our hearts to act a little Job-ish and move us to interrogate God for allowing this chain of events to occur.

Surely, we can sympathize with David and his men after reading of the peril they faced, and I am sure none of us would desire to trade our story with theirs. However, there are some of us who can probably relate with a summation of some disturbing turn of events from our own personal history. Yet, David's inner turmoil was confounded once he found himself unable to mourn with his men because they had turned their backs on him.

First rejection, then dejection, an enormity of distress, and then isolation from the men he served in battle with, the only others who shared the same emotional turmoil, yet they were unable to mourn together as brothers and draw comfort from one another. This had to add insult to all those injuries inflicted on David's heart, mind, and soul, when trusted comrades felt the only salve that would soothe their hurting souls was his death. I have witnessed some challenging times, my friend, but nothing quite like this in a short span of days.

How do you deal with an overload of cascading woes that seem to mount with each passing day? Do you curse God? Do you curse your men and match insult with insult? How do you handle this emotionally charged situation that is able to drain all your willpower and dampen your spirit? That is the inevitable challenge. Keep living long enough and you will discover the "can'ts" of life. You can't control how others react to you, you can't control the curveballs life throws your way, and you can't control the cards you are dealt. But you can control your reaction to every situation you find yourself in. And for David, with his back against a wall, stuck between a rock and a hard place, he chose to handle a terrible situation by living life forward and encouraging himself. He didn't waste his pain.

David couldn't return to Israel. He couldn't rely on his friend, King Achish; he couldn't rely on his family or children, and he certainly couldn't rely on his men. But rather than implode or quit, David chose to keep fighting. How do you fight on when all hope seems gone? Like David, you find help in the hope of self-encouragement.

"But David strengthened himself in the LORD his God." (1 Sam 30:6)

Now don't confuse this with self-help, because the verse does not tell us he reached down deep within himself, relying on inner fortitude to discover help for his soul. We are shown instead, although he encouraged and strengthened himself, that he did this by turning to the One that "… will never leave you nor forsake you" (Hebrews 13:5 ESV). David didn't dwell on the misery of the moment, nor did he recount the troubling experience of the last three days of his life. He took the route of a person who intends to win when others feel winning is impossible. He turned to the Lord because he took comfort in trusting that God was still in control of the outcome.

"And David said to Abiathar the priest, the son of Ahimelech, 'Bring me the ephod.' So Abiathar brought the ephod to David. And David inquired of the LORD. "Shall I pursue after this band? Shall I overtake them?'" (1 Sam 30:7-8)

At the moment when life has dealt you the poorest possible hand, when the only likely choice is to give up, do yourself a solid and look up. Because that's where the real help comes from. Scripture reminds us, "God is our strength, a very present help in trouble" (Psalm 46:1 ESV).

During an awful stretch of David's life, when most people would dismiss their faith in God, David kept a short-term memory of his misery and a long-term account of his Master. In the darkest moments when it seems there is no hope, resist abandoning your faith and execute the same move as David. Turn to God; rely on Him.

Notice the absence of daily lamenting on David's part in scripture. You don't see where David spent a whole lot of time wallowing in self-pity or languishing in his pain. David doesn't take this opportunity to call Achish out for failing to succeed in his attempt to convince the men he was faithful. The way David moved from lament to leading the charge to fight for his family makes you wonder if David had been in some tough situations before.

Facing a bear head on. Tough! Fighting with a mean hungry lion all alone? Tough! Being a young boy standing in the arena with a giant of a man almost ten feet tall, with only three smooth stones and a sling shot to fight with? Tough! But each time, David never stood *alone*.

Your servant has struck down both lions and bears, and this uncircumcised Philistine shall be like one of them, for he has defied the armies of the living God. And David said, "The LORD who delivered me from the paw of the lion and from the paw of the bear will deliver me from the hand of this Philistine." (1 Sam 17:36-37)

This is how you face the giants in your life and win. "The God that guided David guides you. You simply need to consult your maker."[8] This is how you defeat self-doubt. This is how you move from misery and pain to conquering the game of life. Keep short-term accounts of your painful past and long-term accounts of the One who gives you hope, because He is your truest help. Has God delivered you before? Has He brought you over and brought you out of some trying times? Can you look back over your life and attest, "if it had not been for the Lord on my side…?"

Recall how God brought you through the last storm and encourage yourself with this reminder: "Jesus Christ is the same yesterday and today and forever" (Hebrews 13:8 ESV). Instead of losing hope because life seems too hard, look yourself in the mirror and decide, "With God on my side, I can play the hand I am dealt. I may not like the turn of events, but with God, I can go on. I don't have all the answers to overcoming my sorrow, but I can choose to deal with it because I have surrendered my life to the Most-High God who holds tomorrow."

Self-encouragement is the positive energy everyone must learn to use if we are to fight against all odds during the most difficult periods of our lives. This is not a call for self-reliance or self-help revitalization. My intent is not to signal a need to become audacious instead of trusting God and believing in prayer. On the contrary. Self-encouragement is not devoid of God.

Continue to Operate in Your Gift: Use your Gift Even During Setbacks

One of the biggest mistakes we tend to make once life knocks us off course is to ground our goals, desert our dreams, shelve our gifts, leaving little room for a comeback. No matter the situation that caused the setback, giving up is not the best choice to make.

Take Samson's life, for example. Samson's unfortunate end was precipitated by his failure to perform his intended mission according to the will of God. God sent Samson to destroy the Philistines and instead he chose to enjoy the company of the Philistines. Samson failed to see that his gift of superhuman strength was granted by God to use for God's purpose on the earth. Samson began to take pride in his gift, thus claiming it as his own. This caused Samson to become complacent and mentally weak, though remaining physically strong. Samson became comfortable living with the enemy because his pride told him he was invincible, convincing him he could toy with his enemies simply because they feared his strength.

Little did Samson know, the one enemy not afraid of him was the one he allowed to become too close to him, resulting in her eventually outwitting him. In her hands, Samson became the pawn in her chess game, instead of the other way around. This is a warning to us all. Work your intended assignment with fear and awe of the Lord, simply because whatever gift you are operating in, you didn't derive, create or grant; your gift was provided by God Almighty. Being gifted or talented should not cause us to walk in pride and arrogance. Being gifted should cause us to develop a state of humility and reverence toward the One that gifted us in the first place. The best attitude a gifted person can have is one of humility simply because "The LORD gave, and the LORD has taken away…" (Job 1:21 ESV).

The gifted should always check in with God to ensure they are walking out the assigned purpose God placed on their life. When my children graduated from high school, my wife and I suggested they reserve the right to spend any monetary gifts they received on college-related expenses.

Although they had the right to spend their money any way they desired, there was indeed a greater use for the gifts they received. The same is true with the gifts and talents God endows us with as his creation. *Although we are the custodians of the gift, we should never lose sight of the fact that the giver had a greater purpose for intended.*

This is where Samson's troubles started; he failed to acknowledge the giver of his gift and the fact that his gift had a greater purpose; greater than being pretentious and making sport of his enemies. Greater than being arrogant and living invincible in enemy territory. A greater purpose that demanded Samson to seek God's guidance in governing his gift.

But Samson betrayed the purpose of his gift, only to eventually lose it and fall into the hands of his enemy. The good news is that Samson discovered he served a God who willingly and graciously bestows another chance upon his children. Samson was able to rebound from his previous failures because God did not treat Samson the way his sins deserved. The once-mighty Samson who failed to use his gift wisely was able to fail forward and put his trust in the Almighty God.

Can God trust you to fulfill your gift's purpose even though life has been difficult? One person who was surely no stranger to overcoming turmoil while planning for a great future was Joseph, the earthly father of Jesus. Yet, Joseph persevered. He remained faithful to Mary and faithful to his calling by raising Jesus as his own son. We don't often think of the difficult struggle Joseph faced by finding out Mary was pregnant while engaged to become his wife. We don't often sympathize with Joseph for having to deal with feelings of betrayal by his beloved Mary, yet refusing to expose her publicly for her perceived infidelity. He instead protected her reputation and character, suffering in silence.

Although the bible informs us that Joseph struggled with his decision of how to resolve his unexpected dilemma, he hesitated to overreact, leaving room for God's work. God worked on his behalf by sending an angel to provide the answer to his problem.

Make no mistake, Joseph and Mary's life didn't become easier after the angel's revelation to Joseph; certainly, their life became more difficult going forward. Surely, they faced public scorn and ridicule by family, friends, and those from their inner circle as they wondered who fathered Mary's illegitimate child. Why didn't Joseph divorce her for her infidelity? Undoubtedly, the uncertainty of being responsible for raising the Son of God must have added another level of drama to the difficult reality Joseph already faced. Given all the emotional turmoil he must have experienced, despite the gossip, stares, and uncertainty, he still remained devoted, never wavering from his calling.

If anyone had reason to abandon a plan of marrying the love of his life, desert his dream of raising a family with his bride to be, or become discouraged, no longer seeing Mary as a gift from God, Joseph was that man. Despite the difficult situation he faced and monumental decision he had to make, Joseph trusted God. I ask you again, can God trust you to remain faithful to your calling and operate in your gift despite your previous pain and disappointments? Or will you continue to succumb to the pain, lose hope, and turn your back on your calling because you feel your dreams were dashed, and dealing with uncertainty is too much to bear?

Before you decide, consider two notable athletes who faced challenges early in life while pursuing their dreams. These men are easily considered two of the greatest professional basketball players of all time. However, if either of them had allowed adversity of the moment to prevail during their youth, neither would have been included among the greatest in the sport of basketball.

Ask most basketball fans how many championships Michael Jordan won, and they would probably provide the answer with sufficient details of his games. However, not many fans know that Jordan had to overcome feelings of not being as good as his peers, because he did not make the varsity roster in high school, finding himself on junior varsity instead. Imagine that; the great, high flying, Mister Clutch, Michael Jordan, didn't make the cut during his first shot at being on the varsity squad in high school.

Larry Bird was one of the players responsible for returning the Boston Celtics to prominence, and is always recognized for his tenacity and prowess on the court during his playing days. He is also hailed as one of the greatest players of all time. Bird and the Celtics gave fans some of the most memorable championship series against the Lakers and Magic Johnson. Even before he reached the NBA, Bird and Indiana State played Michigan State and Erving Johnson in the 1979 NCAA championships game, giving fans a taste of what was to come on their way to the NBA.

Yet, few fans know Bird started his college career at Indiana under the great coach Bobby Knight, only to leave school before the start of the season and eventually enroll in Indiana State because he felt he didn't fit in at Indiana. Most up and coming young ball players from the Midwest would have been honored to allow Bobby Knight to mold and shape their raw basketball skills and turn them into exceptional players on the road to the NBA. Given, his decision to leave without seeing if he could make the team could have seriously affected Bird and derailed his basketball career. Instead, he set records at Indiana State, leading them to their best season and winning the NCAA championship his senior year.

How did Bird and Jordan excel despite their early setbacks? How did they overcome the meddling mental misery of the moment and go on to become two of the most celebrated marquee names in their profession? Simple, they remained dedicated to their goals and devoted to their dream. I believe disappointment fed their yearning to become the best and made them work even harder. I have never met these two men, but I believe they used the adversity of their respective trials to fuel their drive to succeed and prove the doubting thoughts of their own minds wrong.

Before you dismiss their ability to overcome their personal obstacles because they were great basketball players, keep in mind that a personal goal is just that, someone's desire to succeed where they feel called or led in life. If these men could allow adversity to pave their road to success, what about you, and what about me? Don't allow challenges or setbacks to sink you or cause you to stumble. Use each hurdle as a steppingstone to rise. Trust God and keep dreaming.

Trust God: God's Grace Overrules Our Failures

In the story of Samson, God's grace obviously allowed Samson to finish his mission. Because Samson placed so much trust in himself, he left out the need to trust God, leaving himself unguarded against the secret weapon his enemy had in Delilah.

But he turned to God during his unfortunate circumstances and placed full trust in God, not in himself. God showed Samson something you and I must eventually come to know about our God as well. His grace is bigger than any mistake you and I could ever make. This is why we should never ignore or disbelieve the power of God's grace. Turning to God and trusting Him after making a mistake allows His grace to overrule the damage of our failures and present an opportunity for another chance.

Friend, have you turned to God following consequences of your actions? Have you trusted God after your fumbles, flaws, and missed opportunities? I respectfully suggest you rush to follow the path of Samson, turn to God, and place your total trust in Him. The Bible teaches us in Proverbs 3:5-6 to, "Trust in the Lord with all our hearts and lean not to our own understanding; in all our ways acknowledge Him and He will make our paths straight." That's exactly what Samson did, and that is exactly what you and I need to do.

Samson didn't allow bad circumstances to make him bitter the way many of us do. He never turned on the toxic fountain many people choose to tap into. Once that happens, turning the fountain off is never easy. Resist the desire to complain; use that energy to play your hand. Don't waste your pain.

Playing the Hand You Are Dealt: Don't Sweat the Cards You Receive

The game is Spades, the big joker and the little joker are included as trump cards; the deuce of diamonds and the deuce of spades are wild. Playing off-suit instead of a trump card is reneging, causing your team to forfeit at least one book previously won. The dealer passes out the cards and everyone starts aligning their cards in their hands. If you watch and listen carefully, some players give away their hand by the sounds they make and their facial expressions, while others have learned the art of the poker face (no expression at all).

Some of the most satisfied people in life are those who have learned to play the hand they are dealt. The best players are not necessarily those who hold the better cards. Instead, they are those who have learned to never sweat the cards they receive during the game. They realize that each player is dealt the same number of cards, required to play by the same rules, and each must try to capitalize on what they have in their own hand. For those games that allow partners, players realize they must rely on their partner's hand sometimes when the cards they have don't offer an advantage.

Well, I contend that life is the same way, my friends. There are so many variables beyond our control: parents, birthplace, siblings, economic beginnings, etc. However, everyone must decide if they will sweat life's uncontrollable circumstances or simply make the best of what is before them, no matter the particulars. Play the hand you are dealt. I believe the primary reason why some of us never reach the consciousness to play the hand we are dealt and live a satisfied life is because we end up bitten by the bug of comparison. This happens when we focus on a contrived ratio of "have and have nots". Before we realize it, we start displaying symptomatic behavioral patterns of always comparing ourselves with others. As time goes on, the comparison bug's venom starts to affect our minds, and we transition from simply comparing our lives with others to believing that life is unfair and the hand we are dealt justifies us becoming bitter, constantly complaining. This is a tremendously draining mistake—subjection to self-inflicting harm.

We can always find someone with something bigger, faster, better, or more expensive. Comparing yourself with others will always lead to your cards looking less attractive and insufficient, keeping you from being a winner. Instead of learning to win with what looks like an average hand, we toss in or misplay hand after hand because of our warped perception and inability to adjust.

To make matters worse, once a person starts down this rabbit hole of delusional thinking, they never seem to recover and are left believing everyone else's hand or life is better than their own. They develop a mindset that God apparently favors others. Try as you may, you will have a most difficult time convincing them they have to play the hand they are dealt to improve their opportunities; to become winners despite the odds.

The reality is, once we become fixated on the lives of others, we lose the ability to focus on ourselves and what we have going on. This constant comparison diminishes creative energy and ability to focus. Unfortunately, many are unable to shift out of this line of thinking, thus wasting mental energy; invariably idolizing and envying the life that others live.

Yet, the one concept we need to exercise that will change our lives is the last act we are willing to execute. Playing the had we are dealt. Performing this simple act will have a definite impact. We will discover playing our own hand with excellence and worrying about the hand someone else was dealt is hard to achieve. Play our own hand takes a certain amount of concentration, and attention to detail we cannot ignore. This is the significance of playing our own hand.

If you desire to develop the skills to win at life, you must train your mind to avoid comparison and focus on your own hand. This is the key that unlocks the secret door of contentment. I am certain the apostle Paul made this shift when he stated these life-altering words, "…for I have learned in whatever situation I am to be content" (Philip 4:11 ESV).

Being content is the secret sauce that added to life that enables us to stomach the most unpalatable situations we are force-fed in life. Paul learned to navigate the circumstances of life, through the low valleys as well as the high peaks, and never arrive at the point of making comparisons. Living with a heart of contentment allowed Paul to face the most extreme circumstances feeling empowered to succeed. Paul played the hand he was dealt, overcoming the lowest moments in life. I am a firm believer that we can all accomplish the same if we remain focused.

Never Fail to Give Thanks

When I was a child, my parents made a big deal about giving thanks (saying grace) at the dinner table before my siblings and I were allowed to chow down. Everyone at the dinner table was afforded the opportunity to offer a word of thanks to God for the food we were about to receive. Mostly my mom, or sometimes my sisters spent hours prepping and cooking, making sure the food tasted scrumptious for the most finicky food critic in the room, usually me.

My favorite words of thanksgiving from scripture had nothing whatsoever to do with the meal. My thanksgiving words were always "Jesus wept" (John 11:35). Could this explain why most of the time I was the one who failed to eat all my food and summoned to memory the meal my neighbors were having instead?

Jesus did weep. However, His weeping never made me see the advantage of having a table full of food prepared by the loving hands of my own dear mom. I was busy feeling ungrateful for the blessings of my table. I failed to give proper thanks to a giving God for the food and the family I had around my own table, sharing a nourishing meal in my parents' home. That was my childhood self.

Permit me to ask you, what's your problem? When you fail to properly take inventory of all that God has provided for you, you are acting just like I did, as an ungrateful child. Nothing you have you rightfully deserve. Anything you need, your God can provide. Ray Pritchard was right: "Gratitude is another mark that you are a child of God. All that you have, including life itself, comes from God. Take time daily to say "Thank You" to God for all His blessings. This will keep you from becoming hard and bitter when things don't go your way."[9]

When we were young, our guardians had to teach us how to say "thank you" by prompting us when someone did something nice for us or gave us something, no matter how big or small the act of kindness. Hopefully, we took that into adulthood and we are currently practicing those lessons and teaching them to our own children.

Think back to a time when you became so elated by a specific gift you received that no one needed to prompt you to say thanks. That's exactly how we should live our lives towards God, who has given us the best that He had to give, Jesus Christ.

My childhood self is a constant reminder that the failure to give God His just thanks for life in general is the reason why we are unable to live with gratitude and contentment. I am reminded of the lyrics of this song that reads:

> Give thanks with a grateful heart
> Give thanks to the Holy One
> Give thanks because He's given Jesus Christ, His Son[10]

These lyrics contend with us that we have so much to give God thanks for, and when we do, we should always offer our thanks with a heart filled with gratitude towards such a giving God; thankful if for nothing else than giving us His son, Jesus Christ.

Have you thanked God for His goodness towards you lately? Why don't you take a moment and just bless Him for the life you don't deserve and for the blessings you don't own? God is indeed worthy of our praise.

Show Gratitude

There are always people who have less and people who have more of the material blessings we too often covet. Yet, those who have less many times live life more fully than the people who have "more". This correction will aid you in living life forward and playing the hand you are dealt. Give thanks, act grateful, show gratitude to God just for giving you life.

When was the last time you woke up and first thing in the morning shouted, "Thank you, God, for a new day!"?

"Thank you for protecting me all night long, allowing your angels to keep watch over my family and me as we slept."

When was the last time you thanked God for having a roof over your head, clothes on your back, and food on your table?

We have so much to thank God for and yet, we waste most of our time during the day complaining as if we have nothing to thank God for at all. Ingratitude robs us of our right to serve Him as His people. One of the byproducts of gratitude is thanksgiving. Although you can give thanks without being grateful, you cannot have gratitude without being moved to give thanks. The words "have an attitude of gratitude" sound cute, but there is much more to their meaning. The seed of gratitude is planted once we are mindful of all God has done for us, which eventually brings forth a shout of thanksgiving from our lips as well as our hearts. The songwriter was correct: "When I think of the goodness of Jesus and all he has done for me, my soul, my soul cries out Hallelujah, hallelujah, I thank God for saving me."[11]

When we think back to where we were when God saved us and imagine how dreadful our lives would have turned out if He had left us where he found us, every believer's heart should intimately overflow with gratitude towards God. This should stir a burning desire to praise God when we consider our former lives. Former life meaning the way we used to live, the places we go, the people we used to associate with, and the sins we used to willfully commit. Our former life—when we were lost and trapped as slaves to sin.

Now that we've been saved for a while, we no longer consider salvation as the most precious gift. Instead we are caught up in temporal blessings that fade, break down, and eventually wear out. No longer is God enough, no longer are we blessed because Christ is our Savior, no longer is being a child of God the path to living our best life. Somewhere between salvation and living we have allowed the bitter root of ingratitude to steal our joy.

Ingratitude serves as a deceptive thief, suggesting that whatever we have isn't enough, therefore we can forfeit that which we must make room for more. Walter Hawkins' perfectly penned lyrics should serve as a reminder, no matter the circumstances we should live gratefully:

> God desires to feel your longing,
> Every pain that you feel.
> He feels them just like you (just like you);
> But He can't afford to let you feel only good (only good).
> Then you can appreciate the good times.
> Be grateful, (be grateful)
> Because there's someone else who's worse off than you.
> Be grateful (be grateful)
> Because there's someone else who'd love to be in your shoes
> Be grateful (be grateful)[12]

Amazing how we complain about what we have when someone else would receive our little with open arms. The car we complain about, someone is praying for while riding public transportation. The job we bemoan going to, when someone would trade standing in the unemployment line for our job any day. The house we declare does not fit our lifestyle, while someone is living in a shelter or on the street.

We have traded gratitude with complaints all the while scripture exalts us to serve, "faithful over a little", I will set you over much, enter into the joy of your master" (Matt 25:21).

Represent Faithfully: Faithfully Manage What God has Provided

When you read the verse, the unstated warning seems apparent: learn to live faithfully over the little you have if you expect God to grant you more.

Faithfully managing whatever God provides us clearly takes a concerted effort, but this is how the good player wins with an average hand when those who have been dealt much better hands sometimes play without faith or gratitude and lose.

The aforementioned verse clearly points to the effort that is required to work diligently the little that seemingly requires a small amount of effort. In order to show we are worthy of being entrusted with much more. When our hearts overflow with the fullness of gratitude, we allow our hands to work without the fear of fumbling the slightest opportunities are allowed to oversee.

What has God given you that you have mismanaged because someone else's bounty seemed bigger than yours? Interesting, how we expect more when we have fumbled the little we were given in the first place. We should first learn to manage the little with excellence, proving we are worthy of the more we complain we deserve.

There were successful high school coaches and coaches who worked at lower tier college football programs before going on to lead prominent Division One teams, because they were faithfully committed to the teams they coached in the beginning. Likewise, there were college coaches who went on to lead National Football League teams because they proved their worth while leading college programs.

There are teachers who have similar success stories, advancing from the classroom to running the front office as principal and eventually, curriculum development. There are bag boys who advance to being store managers at prominent grocery chains. The list goes on and on, but the point remains the same. They were all deemed faithful over the little and eventually set up to have much.

The path to advancement is never complaining; the path to advancement is the commitment we give to small, seemingly insignificant blessings we too often cast aside and forfeit because we demand more. Suggestion: follow the path of least resistance (God's way) and do that which is pleasing in His sight. Give thanks, show gratitude, represent faithfully. This is how you avoid the pitfall of mismanaging the hand you are dealt and learn to play your own hand in life. Allow pain to fuel you. Don't waste your pain.

Section II

Allowing Pain to Fuel You

Chapter 7

Fueled by Pain

Countless people turn their past mistakes into a pivotal platform by which they help others navigate the same pitfalls—setbacks that resulted from a series of bad choices. Listen, the resounding truth is that although you don't have the ability to change the past, instead of repeating it you can repair it. Helping others turns your previous pain into a vehicle for giving hope. This should come easily, because you have spent countless hours rehearsing to yourself how you should have made different choices, and how the outcome would have been different.

Why not help someone else since you can't go back in time? You can save someone else from wasting precious time and assist them in choosing different routes to aid in their success. Becoming a mentor to someone, steering them clear of the same pitfalls you succumbed to in your past, can help to set you free from those past mistakes. There is no better way to make the best of a bad situation than pointing someone else in the right direction. Stop worshiping the idols of your past and work those idols into a pulpit you can stand on to present the truth to someone else. Help dispel the notion that being young requires making regrettable mistakes that will only paralyze your potential and cause you to struggle through life.

I hear you saying, "How does this help me?"

See, in your hands, mistakes can lead to occupational paralysis, but in God's hands, mistakes can become pivotal opportunities. Your choice: you can continue to worship the idols of your past, leading to continual depression and endless misery; or you can refuse to waste any more time having pity on yourself and decide that you have a unique story that is worth sharing so you can serve others. Which will you choose?

Because we expend so much effort recalling the pain of our past, we never allow healing to occur. We become accustomed to fighting for the right to live in pain and misery rather than fighting to leave the draining burden of our past behind us. Sadly, we accept the fact that Christ provides us with new spiritual benefits when we become saved, but we refuse to claim the benefits and live accordingly. Thus, the path we take only leads to prolonged agony and unrest in our minds and souls. One of the reasons we fail to walk in "newness of life" is because we never learned to practice the art of renewing our minds.

Renewing Your Mind: Repent and Break Free

We are creatures of habit, by birth and by choice. Our experiences will certainly follow us on our new journey as believers, unless there is a renewal process to transform our old mentality and former lifestyle. This is what repentance is all about for a Christian. We are told to, "repent therefore, and turn again, that your sins may be blotted out, so that times of refreshing may come from the presence of the Lord" (Acts 3:19 DBT).

Repentance means to change your mind about the way you once processed your association and involvement with sin, altering the way sin is perceived and understood, which leads to changing your ways. We must learn to see sin the way God does to break free from our old ways of living. Once this happens, repentance requires one to change their allegiance to sin and align with Jesus Christ.

Both repentance and renewing of the mind play essential roles in a Christian's life. Failing to act on either will leave the person in an unregenerate state, living as if they have no relationship with Christ, as if they have never been saved from their sins in the first place.

However, renewing of the mind allows a person to operate in their repented state by allowing the Word of God to prevail in their life, to pervade their thoughts and govern their actions. Once a caterpillar goes through metamorphosis and turns into a butterfly, significant changes take place. The butterfly, once something rather detestable, transforms to a creature of beauty, desirable for gazing while in flight. The butterfly does not consider its former self. Following its transformation from a lowly caterpillar, the butterfly is free to enjoy a new life.

Renewing your mind is one of the most important links to the Christian faith, which exposes why some exemplify their claim of spiritual transformation while others merely declare their association with Christ. One group clearly shows outward signs of an inward change while the other group is still caught in the same endless cycle as before their conversion.

Trying to live out the Christian faith without renewing your mind is like trying to load new software on a hard drive and forgetting to reboot your computer. In other words, there is a final step that must take place regardless of everything else that has already happened in the installation process. You may recall the when and where of the exact moment you installed the new software, but it will not work without a reboot. The reboot is required.

You see, although the new software has been installed, the old application must be written over or the hardware will only access the old program. Therefore, you must first reboot your computer, for the overwrite to take place. It is the same when we renew our minds; our old way of thinking is overwritten by new thoughts—thoughts of peace and not dread.

Rest assured, there is an obvious connection between the mind and the transformational journey after a person has accepted Christ as their savior.

For scripture declares, "Do not conform to the pattern of this world, but be transformed by the renewing of your mind. Then you will be able to test and approve what God's will is—his good, pleasing, and perfect will." (Romans 12:2 ESV) The mind presents an obvious dilemma for believers when they accept the Lord Jesus as their personal savior. Their hearts now belong to the Lord, their identities are characterized by their association and assimilation with Christ, but their minds are polluted by past experiences with the world. Living with a new heart yet pollution in the head poses a lifestyle malfunction. The part of Romans 12:2 suggests if the mind does not change then continual conformity to the world's system is sure to continue.

If that was not cause enough, just realize that when we fail to renew our minds, we accept Christ but fail to enjoy all the benefits of being in Christ. We forfeit peace, joy, and the guidance that is ours through the Holy Spirit. All these benefits become ours the moment we become saved; however, we must renew our minds to experience each benefit. Cycling back to our illustration of the caterpillar becoming a beautiful butterfly, you will never see a butterfly act as if it were still a caterpillar, crawling on the ground. No, as far as the butterfly knows, it has always been a butterfly, able to float on air and soar to heights far above all the previous problems it encountered as a caterpillar. There is no way a butterfly would return to its former life as a caterpillar. We can surmise the caterpillar has repented and renewed its mind.

The same should ring true in the life of a believer who has accepted Christ. Returning to the old ways of living should repulse, disturb, and trouble the believer. Only then are they able to walk in step with scripture that declares, "I have been crucified with Christ. It is no longer I who live, but Christ lives in me. And the life I now live in the flesh I live by faith in the Son of God, who loved me and gave himself for me." Galatians 2:20 ESV

With a new transformation, we experience the new life we have gained. Don't waste your pain.

Chapter 8

Avoid the Pain

Living life with an unforgiving heart is like walking around sticking a pin in your own heart every time you think about the wrong committed against you. Failing to forgive has caustic ramifications for the one who refuses to forgive, not the one that was never forgiven. When we hesitate to forgive, we end up wounding ourselves instead of harming the other person. Most of the time, the perpetrator of the offense fails to recall the event in question.

We are the only ones that recall the offense in "living color", all too clearly. Carrying this emotional baggage only harms the victim all over again while the victimizer lives with a clear conscience. Yet, here we are, burdening ourselves with painful emotional thoughts. We cannot sleep, eat, or stop thinking of the injustice we suffered. How could so-and-so treat me like this? Why did this happen to me? Why do they have the right to live their lives emotionally free while I continue to suffer from the emotional scars they inflicted?

These are valid questions. However, do not expect any direct answers. This line of questioning only proves you are stuck, and the more time you waste with unproductive questions, the more embedded you become in your own emotional turmoil.

You were hurt. True that! No one is questioning whether you suffered emotionally or possibly physically. The point is you cannot undo the past and living with unforgiveness will not help heal your emotional wounds. My focus is to move you forward to a place of healing, prevent you from continuously suffering unnecessarily by rehashing your painful experiences.

How can you move forward and reverse the course of your life? Simply by elevating your focus and developing a heavenly gaze. What I mean is this, "Set your mind on things that are above, not on things that are on earth." These are exactly the words and mindset Paul tried to instill in the Colossian church, in his letter as recorded in Chapter 3 verse 2 of Colossians. In short, if you desire to avoid living and reliving painful experiences, you first need to start by redirecting your focus from earth toward heaven.

Having an earthly gaze results in a disturbing viewpoint because your vision is distorted by obstacles, barriers, and mountains of trouble as far as the eye can see. However, when you shift your gaze towards the heavens, you start to observe the splendor and majesty of an Almighty God rather than your meager problems. I realize there are times when life seems like an unsolvable puzzle with missing pieces just to annoy and frustrate us to give up and quit.

Then there are occasions where our struggles appear to represent a complicated movie mystery, filled with twists and multiple turns with endless cliffhangers. Now, if you follow the illustrations, then you see how this could fill anyone's heart with anxiety and minds with distress. As anxiety and distress were not enough to overwhelm us, here comes doubt, worry, fear and despair to join in on the party. However, if you read the 6th Chapter of the Gospel according to the writer Matthew, you will discover that most basic struggles center around our approach to life. My point has been reflected going back some thousands of years as well as in the here and now.

Man has always been proven selfish and self-centered, only concerned about self-aggrandizement. Recall if you will, the bible records in the book of Genesis: Eve was enticed to sin by the notion that she could become like God rather than simply being reserved to serve God. See, the heart of man has always desired to become elevated up to God's throne, seeking equality with God rather than a position of humility under God. However, when the heart of man is thus renewed in Christ, we gladly and willingly pronounce ourselves servants of the Most High King.

We are all seeking a number of things out of life and people: accommodation, affirmation, approval, appreciation, praise, happiness; the list goes on and on. Hence the continuum of our pursuit and the never-ending cycle we find impossible to avoid. Unfortunately, none of the things we routinely seek provide any lasting satisfaction or long-term benefits.

After examining our habitual, empty earthly practices, Jesus offers a more excellent journey of unparalleled satisfaction that cannot be duplicated on earth—the kingdom of heaven. As if to say, don't waste your time pursuing useless, unsatisfactory things; instead make heaven and heavenly living the "main thing". After warning against worrying needlessly about the cares of this life, Christ provides the ultimate relief for those who suffer with this problem.

Basic creature comforts are often overly pursued, only drawing us away from more important matters. I like this because it places the significance of life's central purpose not on self, but primarily on God. When we learn to elevate our gaze, we can change our perspective and eventually avoid unnecessary pain.

Erect Monuments to God: Worship God, Not Your Pain

If you don't accept my story, then accept Jacob's story. Become acquainted with it because Jacob's life displays a transition from idolizing self to worshiping God. If ever someone's life appeared as a contradiction in terms, Jacob's early life would qualify. Undoubtedly, Jacob experienced some challenging circumstances as he wrestled with life. However, through all of his ordeals he never abandoned God. Instead, Jacob worshipped God instead of his pain by making a habit of erecting monuments to God. The best way to avoid worshiping our past suffering and pain is to place our experience in proper perspective by worshipping God.

Let's discover how Jacob avoided worshiping the pain of his past and worshiping the God that held his future instead. One important fact is that before he was born, Jacob was declared by God to be the chosen one by whom God would birth his people. However, the circumstances of his early life made Jacob sometimes appear as a man with a cursed existence and a bounty on his head, rather than being favored by God.

This is why you can't allow the rough circumstances of life to dictate the person you are meant to become. Only God has the right and authority to tell you who you are and the purpose you will serve, simply because He created you for His own plan. Oddly enough, we become guilty of boxing ourselves in more than others do to us, with negative conclusions based on unfavorable circumstances. Follow this train of thought: try viewing challenges as sparring partners that help prepare us for the more important fights that inevitably come our way. Instead of whining about every hurdle, learn to roll with the punches and prepare for what lies ahead.

Given the circumstances by which Jacob obtained his twin brother Esau's birthright, he became hated and hunted by him. Based on instructions from his mother Rebekah, Jacob went to his uncle Laban and committed to serve him for seven years, to marry Laban's daughter, Rachel. Except, seven years later, his uncle tricked Jacob on his wedding night by allowing his older daughter to sleep with him instead of the one he loved.

Laban decided that Jacob should serve another seven years before he would honor the commitment to give him Rachel. A seven-year initial agreement turned into a fourteen-year contract, only to cover the original terms. Sometimes conflict is necessary to birth the change that has been lying dormant within us for many years.

The bible indicates an unlikely chance encounter Jacob had one day, wrestling with an unknown man. In the narrative, Jacob suggests the person he wrestled all night was God Himself. Now I must admit, trying to fathom this possibility throws us for a loop. *May I suggest that you don't waste time trying to conceptualize, and just draw that ultimately our fights are not with man, but with God.*

Allow me to try to unravel this thought and add a bit of clarity. A person loses a loved one unexpectedly, and they turn and wrestle with God.

"Where were you?"

"Why did you?"

"How could you?"

Words a grieving person can only hurl in God's direction.

A person loses a job or has some other unfortunate event suddenly occur, and guess who receives an earful? You guessed right, God.

Although our fights start out as battle royales against the world, the last two standing are always God and us. Even though our lives don't display this reality—the fact that God is sovereign—life seems to draw us into a wrestling match only with Him. At some point in our lives, we all end up fighting with God.

The bad news is that we wrestle with God for the wrong reasons. See, this is why I suggest that you become acquainted with Jacob. Jacob didn't waste his encounter; he made the best of his fight with God by asking for a blessing rather than demanding an explanation.

"And Jacob was left alone. And a man wrestled with him until the breaking of the day. When the man saw that he did not prevail against Jacob, he touched his hip socket, and Jacob's hips was put out of joint as he wrestled with him. Then he said, "Let me go, for the day had broken." But Jacob said, "I will not let you go unless you bless me." Genesis 32:24-26 ESV

Our problem is, we haven't matured enough to know that God doesn't owe us anything, let alone an explanation; but He is still in the blessing business.

Jacob's approach was the right approach. He was in a bad position, once again. He was a hunted and hated man. Although he prospered at the hands of God, he was not at peace because he was constantly looking over his shoulder for enemies made through encounters with his brother and uncle. Jacob had grown tired of running, but he realized that he may have run out of tricks to deal with a showdown with his brother, Esau.

During his fight with God, Jacob realized the only one that could provide him a blessing, a way out, a winning resolution, was God Himself. There were no tricks, no one-upping his opponent this time; no, he understood he only needed God to bless his life. Jacob realized before he faced his next opponent, his life needed a fresh transition that only God could provide.

Have you come to the same realization? Are you tired of fighting and losing? Does it feel like as soon as one battle ends, another begins? Once Jacob grew tired of fighting and surrendered his life to God, he recognized that God deserved all the credit for his deliverance, since without God's intervention he could not deliver himself. This realization prompted Jacob to honor God and his newfound reliance on God by erecting a monument so he would never forget.

When we make this same shift to relying on God, we should do the same in our own hearts and minds so we will always remember, if we "acknowledge Him, He shall make straight your paths." (Proverbs 3:6b)

Remember God's Presence: Turn to God

Once you develop the spiritual muscle-memory of worshipping God during your trials, remembering God's presence becomes second nature. The lesson I am trying to teach you is in this life you better have a "same God shout" in your repertoire, because no matter how well you try to prepare and live your life, you are going to face some pain and some rain. Whether you live like a wise person or a fool, you are sure to see some disappointments and some setbacks, some trials and difficult times. This is just one unsettling fact of life.

However, I can tell you from personal experience that when life starts putting the old squeeze on you, when storms come up unexpectedly and you seem to face more rain than sunshine, that's when you need to recall God's presence the most. Listen, stay with me, when you are experiencing a difficult moment, the best prescription for pain relief is to recall God's presence. Look closely at Jacob's life again, to see how this is best accomplished.

In Chapter 32 of the book of Genesis, we catch up with Jacob having just narrowly escaped his uncle Laban's wrath, only to end up facing a showdown with his brother, Esau. At least fourteen years had passed since Jacob last saw Esau, and he still recalled the hatred his brother had for him. Knowing he had to encounter Esau on his journey home caused Jacob great anxiety and fear.

This is a lesson, to realize that there are some confrontations we simply can't avoid. Nonetheless, you still can take comfort knowing God is on your side. The bible tells us that Jacob was, "greatly afraid and distressed" (Genesis 32:7), realizing he could not avoid his brother on his journey, so he devised a plan to prevent great loss to his family while he pondered how to save his own life. What he did next is exactly what I expect a man with developed spiritual muscles to do.

Out of his deep distress and overwhelming fear, Jacob humbled himself and called on God for protection. This was a sign of spiritual maturity; he didn't turn to tricks, to his wit or his desert smarts. He turned to God.

And Jacob said, "O God of my father Abraham and God of my father Isaac, O LORD who said to me, 'Return to your country and to your kindred, that I may do you good. I am not worthy of the least of all the deeds of steadfast love and all the faithfulness that you have shown to your servant, for with only my staff I crossed the Jordan, and now I have become two camps. Please deliver me form the hand of Esau, for I fear him, that he may come and attack me, the mothers with the children. But you said, 'I will surely do you good, and make your offspring as the sand of the sea, which cannot be numbered for multitude." Genesis 32:9-12

Like Jacob, when we remember God's presence, we will experience this wonderful truth: *"God is our refuge and strength, a very present help in the time of trouble."* Psalm 46:1 ESV

Recall God's Goodness: Praise God

All too often we allow negative, traumatic circumstances to delete what we know and have saved in our memory banks of the goodness of God. This allows the situation we are experiencing to precipitate us into a downward emotional and spiritual spiral, invariably causing us to suffer greatly and postpone recovery. However, the truth is we could rather easily avoid this destructive spiral by practicing one thing.

What's that, you ask? Simple, the common practice we should adopt is recalling God's goodness. Instead of creating an atmosphere of doubt, panic, and worry by focusing solely on the impossible situation, we should recall God's goodness.

One day, long ago, Joshua, God's chosen leader to replace Moses, was addressing the children of God. In his address, he reminded the leaders and all the people that his God had delivered them from Egypt, protected them in the wilderness, fought for them when they were attacked by others, and sustained them while they were roaming the desert. Following Joshua's stirring address, he challenged the Israelites to either turn away from the evil practice of idol worship and serve the Lord or continue with their evil ways, but to decide one or the other.

Joshua then made a statement that confirmed his faith in the Almighty God. Joshua Chapter 24, verse 15 states: "But as for me and my house, we will serve the LORD." I believe that Joshua's commitment fostered a shift in the mind of the people who were gathered before him that day, because following his statement, they made their own statement of faith and commitment to God. This is what they said in response to him as recorded in Joshua Chapter 24, verse 16 and 17: "Then the people answered, 'Far be it from us that we should forsake the Lord to serve other gods, for it is the LORD our God who brought us and our fathers up from the land of Egypt, out of the house of slavery, and who did those great signs in our sight and preserved us in all the way that we went, and among all the peoples through whom we passed.' "

I find it most interesting that these words were transformative, yet these were the same people who had turned their backs on God in the first place. They had obviously failed to follow and serve God prior to Joshua's address. But notice what they stated as the reason for making their decision—that God was responsible for delivering them and their fathers over the years. The point is, recalling God's goodness immediately erases bad practices and allows us to replace those practices with good and productive behavior, which can serve to abort our downward emotional spiral. When they thought of the goodness of God, they realized the only one that deserved their worship was the one that had delivered them in the past.

Though in the past they had failed to worship God and served other gods, their recall of God's goodness caused a renewed commitment to honor, serve, and worship Him. This is the practice we need to adopt for ourselves; the events that occurred in their lives were not pleasant. They were enslaved in Egypt and once released, encountered danger from every surrounding nation. Do you get the point? Even though their path was not paved or easy, they still had reason to celebrate the goodness of God.

This celebratory outbreak allows us to work our way through trials while God delivers us once again. Recalling God's goodness provides us from wallowing in the misery of the situation and keeps us focused more on what God is able to do than on what we are going through. Focusing on God's goodness provides us with a constant drum beat of the fact that the same God that brought us through the last impossible dilemma is more than able to bring us through again.

The primary cause of downward spirals is focusing more on the stress, conflict, and tension a problem is causing and less on the goodness of God. The issue is not the timing of the problem; the issue is the timing of our worship. There is nothing called, "the best time for a problem to arise." You and I both know there is never a good time for a problem. By definition, a problem is an untimely, unwelcome situation that introduces a certain level of stress, conflict, and disharmony in a person's current domain.

What's funny is we have even mouthed the words, "I can't believe this is happening right now"—as if any other time we would welcome trouble, but now is not a good time. There will never exist a good time for a problem to arise. Since this is true, the timing of the problem should not monopolize our mental capacity, but instead when the problem arises, we should allow this to kick-start our praise. *The arrival of the problem should cause us to push the pause button on panic and push the play button on praise.*

You will find panicking and praise very difficult to accomplish at the same time and in the same space. So, the correct behavior is to recall the goodness of God when life introduces problematic situations that we are unable to resolve by ourselves.

Rehearse God's Promises: Not Painful Memories

Another practice that relieves the tension of life is to rehearse God's promises. Unfortunately, as human beings we are prone to review and analyze our most difficult moments versus forgetting these moments as quickly as possible. One main cause of this inability to let go of the past is the replay mechanism we all seem to have in common. This replay mechanism is apparently a reflex impulse that roams uncontrollably in our minds causing undue distress if left unchecked. The dilemma is we don't have the ability to switch off this mechanism once it starts.

There is hope. To shut down this rehearsal mechanism, just rehearse God's promises instead of painful memories. As I stated earlier, this reflex impulse causes us to suffer daily, even when we desire for the memory replay to stop. That's the bad news. The good news is replaying God's promises in place of bad memories drowns out the echo of the past ringing in our heads.

It is essential to incorporate this practice daily. Start each day reading a scripture that references God's promises to his children. Greater still, choose a scripture that is conditional upon man fulfilling his duty, culminating in God fulfilling His promise. For example, 2 Chronicles, Chapter 14, verse 7: *"If my people who are called by my name will humble themselves and pray and seek my face and turn from their wicked ways, then will I hear from heaven and forgive their sin and heal their land."*

In this scripture, we can see man's responsibility is highlighted with four different commands to follow. These are then followed by two definite promises of God: forgiveness and healing. This represents an interactive relationship between God and man which results in man receiving the promises of God. Here we notice a direct correlation between man's fulfillment of his responsibilities and God's fulfillment of His promises to man. This correlation emphasizes one important fact, man's relationship with God. This is the big idea of focusing on God's promises, which should become more than a therapeutic exercise but a comforting reminder that we are beneficiaries of an intimate relationship with the God of the universe. And the same God has made wonderful promises to us that should overshadow all the painful memories we are forced to stare down. Thus providing us both comfort and healing for our souls. Incorporating this scripture as an early morning devotional serves to replace painful memories that constantly bombard one's mind with pleasant reminders of God's faithfulness toward us, a wonderful practice of starting each morning focused on God. Live forward. Don't waste your pain.

Chapter 9

Retool and Live

Our lives often resemble the experiences we have been through because we fail to successfully retool along the way. We remain beholden to our past by reviewing yesterday's mistakes as if somehow they will mysteriously disappear or magically be erased. Not only does this wishful thinking produce wasted time and results, but we come away even more bitter and defeated with every merciless visitation of painful yesterdays.

There is indeed wonderful news, a way out for us all. In 1 Kings, Chapter 17, we are given a look at how to take advantage of a concept that I call simply, "retool and live". In this passage of scripture we see first-hand how to put this concept into practice for beneficial results. Let's read what takes place.

7 And after a while the brook dried up, because there was no rain in the land. 8 Then the word of the Lord came to him, 9 "Arise, go to Zarephath, which belongs to Sidon, and dwell there. Behold, I have commanded a widow there to feed you." 10 So he arose and went to Zarephath. And when he came to the gate of the city, behold, a widow was there gathering sticks. And he called to her and said, "Bring me a little water in a vessel, that I may drink, 11 And as she was going to bring it, he called to her and said, "Bring me a morsel of bread in your hand." 12 And she said, "As the Lord your God lives, I have nothing baked, only a handful of flour in a jar and a little oil in a jug. And now I am gathering a couple of sticks that I may go in and prepare it for myself and my son, that we may eat it and die." 13 And Elijah said to her, "Do not fear; go and do as you have said. But first make me a little cake of it and bring it to me, and afterward make something for yourself and your son. 14 For thus says the Lord, the God of Israel, 'The jar of flour shall not be spent, and the jug of oil shall not be empty, until the day that the Lord sends rain upon the earth.'" 15 And she went and did as Elijah said. And she and he and her household ate for many days. 16 The jar of flour was not spent, neither did the jug of oil become empty, according to the word of the Lord that he spoke by Elijah.

1 Kings 17:7-16

In this biblical account of the life of one of God's prophets, we catch up to him during a transitional period. Elijah, the prophet of God has just delivered a message from God to Ahab, the wicked reigning king of Israel. Upon the heels of his confrontational message, Elijah was instructed by God to depart the presence of Ahab and camp out in solitude by a brook in the land of Jordan. While there, God would place him on a supernatural meal plan by sending raven waiters to serve him bread and meat, day and night.

To quench his thirst, Elijah drank from the brook during his stay in Jordan. He did as he was instructed, and all was well until an unfortunate turn of events took place. His good thing ran out; his wonderful meal plan came to a halt, and his setup took a setback. As a result, Elijah had to relocate from his place of comfort in search of a new source of food and water. What I find amazing is how he seemed to take all of this in stride.

In this story, Elijah finds himself in a bad way one day. After relying on a brook to provide him with necessary sustenance for life, it suddenly dried up. This type of unexpected change in life is something that causes God's children much too often to doubt God's love and sovereignty. But we never see Elijah curse God, become distressed, or react negatively to the constant packing and unpacking, having to relocate from town to town. No, Elijah teaches us the quintessential lesson of trusting God through life's transitions. Through the prophet, we observe how maintaining trust in God allows room for God to prove He is indeed able to orchestrate each transitional moment, affording us the opportunity to retool and live forward.

Pray Instead of Panicking: God is UP to Something

Learning to accept our inability to know the mind of God and see into the future, should never cause us to doubt God. We allow our troubles to cause us to transfer our limitations onto God and start panicking instead of walking in faith. This is why Elijah is an excellent example of how to retool and live forward. When unfortunate situations occur, our favorite fallback plan is typically to panic rather than pray, but if we do pray first, the minute we start to evaluate the situation and ascertain just how bad it is, we switch from prayer back to panic mode.

In Elijah's story, the prophet was able to hear clear instructions from God telling him to relocate. Instead of sweating the unfortunate situation he found himself in, instead of complaining about the obvious fact that God let the brook dry up, instead of asking God how he could do something like this if he loved him, he simply trusted God, retooled, and lived forward. By moving on to a different region called Zarephath as God instructed, Elijah was able to realize that God had set him up to receive more than his usual provisions by the hand of a widow in that land. Elijah's life was abruptly disrupted by the lack of rain in the region, forcing him to relocate. Albeit this situation served as a setup for God to increase His provisions towards him in a miraculous way. Yet, to receive increase, he first had to suffer a setback. He had to quickly walk away from his past in the direction of his new beginning. Elijah had to retool.

From his predicament and actions, we learn the first lesson of the advantages gained when able to retool and live forward. Elijah didn't put his faith in the brook; instead he always kept his trust in God. In order to retool, we can never lose our trust in the almighty God.

Don't Languish, Listen: Seize the Opportunity

In life, sudden unfortunate circumstances are bound to occur at one point or another. This is not an "if", but a "when". When these circumstances come knocking, we must adopt the ability to retool and live. God was able to bring to pass an immediate blessing because Elijah didn't waste time rehashing how good he once had it. I believe this behavior is what allowed Elijah to clearly hear God's instructions concerning where his next blessing was coming from.

By not spending time holding a pity party, Elijah was able to maintain his faith and keep the lines of communication open between himself and God. Refusing to allow the sudden change in good favor trigger a sense of entitlement within his heart kept Elijah's dependence upon God firmly established. When God provided him with his relocation orders, he gracefully received and accepted his new transfer.

Every downsize is not a death sentence to your career; every closed door is not a missed opportunity for good fortune; and every dried brook is not a sign that God does not love you or that he is less than capable of blessing you. No, these seemingly bad situations and misfortunes are God setting you up with something bigger, showing just how great and awesome a provider He really is.

If you were hung up on Elijah's bad situation, you may have missed that God's instructions gave him even better news. The dried brook provided a chance for him to receive a home cooked meal from the kitchen of a widow in Zarephath. No more drinking from an outdoor brook and receiving scraps from a raven; he had now been awarded God's Gold Meal Plan, fit for a prophet. All too often we dwell so heavily on the past that we fail to see how good our present circumstances have become.

Now if you analyze verses 10 and 11, you will notice that Elijah meets the lady assigned to provide him his new meal plan. Because of her current circumstances (down to her last meal and running out of cooking supplies), she was preparing for the worst when the prophet arrived on the scene. Elijah being thirsty because he had just experienced a disruption in his water supply, asked for the first thing he lacked, something to quench his thirst. Then he asked for something to eat. I don't want to linger here, but we can learn something from Elijah's understanding of the need to prioritize. Possibly we delay our blessings because we circumvent true needs by seeking secondary blessings first, all because we are confused about what is most important.

By considering God's heart as more important than seeking God's hand, we would end up with both and miss out on neither. Carefully following the example Elijah set provides us with the same opportunity to receive divine blessings simply by listening instead of rushing to "speak negative of and over our current situations." Although Elijah's circumstances took a turn for the worse, he could clearly hear the voice of God leading him to green pastures and still waters (Psalm 23) because he never wasted time making matters worse. He refused to allow mouth "to declare disaster ahead of time"; he refused "to be critical of the situation in advance"[13]. Can you learn this healthy habit and listen for God to lead you through your next storm?

Growth Is Required: Living Life Forward Produces Fruit

In 2008, a movie entitled "The Curious Case of Benjamin Button" was released in theatres across the country with a rather interesting story line. Benjamin Button, the main character, was born with a rare abnormality that caused his body to age in reverse, living life essentially backwards, from old age to infancy. Although the movie was provided for entertainment purposes, it depicted the exact opposite of God's expectation of His children—to live life in one direction. Highly doubtful if I could find a loving parent who would desire for their children to advance in age only to regress, never becoming fully developed mentally or physically. Yet, we seem satisfied as God's children with portraying ourselves as "spiritual

Benjamin Buttons", either because we have relapsed spiritually, remain spiritually underdeveloped, or we have experienced spiritual malnutrition.

Make no mistake, God has the same expectations of His children as any loving parent does, to see us grown and fully spiritually developed. God is so committed to our spiritual growth, He has provided us with the necessary tools to develop as Christians and become more like His Son, every day; assistance designed to prevent us from becoming spiritual Benjamin Buttons and instead, "grow in the grace and knowledge of our Lord and Savior Jesus Christ" (2 Peter 3:18 ESV).

Well, just how will we know when we are growing and maturing as followers of Jesus, or if our spirituality has become stunted somehow? From all we have read and learned from the Bible, one concept is evident—growth is required, and the evidence that we are growing, thriving, and becoming healthy Christians is by the fruit we bear. A scripture reference that explains how results of our growth are evidence of our growth, is as follows:

"Rather, speaking the truth in love, we are to grow up in every way into Him who is the head, into Christ, from whom the whole body, joined together by every joint with which it is equipped, when each part is working properly, makes the body grow so that it builds itself up in love" (Ephesians 4:15-16 ESV).

From the verses we can deduce with assurance that God expects his children to grow, mature, and develop spiritually in Christ. Clearly, the text points out that growth is not something we hope or pray for as Christians, but rather growth is required of us once we accept Jesus as our Lord and Savior. God does not intend for us to remain the same as the way we came to Christ. The problem exists when we allow the valleys, setbacks, disappointments of life to impact us and stunt our spiritual growth, causing us to regress. Thus, being spiritually malnourished leaves us unable to bear much fruit, or at times no fruit at all. Romans 8:29 tells us: *"For those whom he foreknew he also predestined to be conformed to the image of his Son, in order that he might be the firstborn among many brothers."*

God's growth chart for His children is only scaled by our Christlikeness, therefore we should all continue aspiring and striving toward the sole goal, to "grow up in Christ". How we are growing as Christians has more to do with our application of scripture as we interface with others than our interpretation of the word. In fact, scripture informs us that the true indicator of our spiritual growth is revealed in our discourse. In other words, a lack of spiritual maturity is evident when there exists a failure to communicate in a loving way between the saints of God, causing an unacceptable language barrier.

The only way to correct this language barrier is to "speak the truth in love," which represents proof that we are growing in Christ. "In Christ" indicates the growth of a Christian is not independent of Christ, but rather directly dependent upon and related to Christ alone. Our responsibility is to stay committed to the process.

Notice from Ephesians 4:14-15: Christ does not conduct one-on-one growth sessions; instead he develops his children as a unit, as one, specifically as one body—each member depending on the others for growth and support, with the result always being love. If we remain fully connected to His body, we should produce the same level of love He exemplified when He walked the earth years before. Love is the one fruit that reveals we are children of God, becoming fully developed as believers in Jesus Christ. Growth is not only required, but the expectation is we must keep growing to prevent spiritual apathy.

We must avoid the mistake of thinking we can continue to grow spiritually if we become disconnected from the body of Christ. Our connection to the body of Christ is essential for ongoing development if we expect to display Christlikeness—being loving and speaking lovingly towards one another. Invariably, there should be a distinct difference in a grown, mature Christian and a new believer in Christ. Paul provided us with this distinction when he stated:

"When I was a child, I spoke like a child, I thought like a child, I reasoned like a child. When I became a man, I gave up childish ways" (1 Corinthians 13:11 ESV).

There is no denying that at some point in our Christian journey we were very much like young children with respect to our understanding of God, His will, His word, and our walk with the Lord. The phrase, "when I was a child" implies Paul recognized he was no longer the person he once had been; he has now grown into mature adulthood and evolved beyond his spiritual childhood days and ways. Furthermore, he implies he understands his childhood existed in another time that he no longer needs to draw upon as an adult.

Admittedly, there are some good and bad memories we may all recall from our childhood. However, the sad truth is for some there are probably more bad memories that may overshadow and outlast the good. I too, have some memories I would rather not dwell on. Yet, our childhood has a place in our lives, though that place does not have to dictate or determine how we live in the present.

Paul provided help by suggesting there are certain known childhood behaviors that are only relevant during those formative years. He makes the point that during childhood, we can only speak a certain way, think a certain way, and process rational thoughts a certain way, because after all, we are only children. One big mistake guardians and parents make is to seemingly place a higher expectation on children who have not fully matured. Paul discerns that children are limited and underdeveloped in their speech, thinking, and reasoning in comparison to adults. No matter how mature a child seems, their lack of experience limits the wisdom they can draw from, even those who have an inner circle from which they may gain an older glimpse of life.

I am neither suggesting nor denying that experience is the best teacher. I am merely suggesting that *"wisdom is the principal thing; therefore, get wisdom and in all your getting, get understanding"* (Proverbs 4:7 ESV). Meaning, the acquisition of both wisdom and understanding are necessary aspects of life, and both take a certain amount of time for us to gain what childhood experience doesn't allow.

One clear indicator that we have grown up is when we abandon the childlike right or desire to communicate by way of "brutal honesty" and rather "speak the truth in love." Children have an unfiltered innocence that forces them to bluntly share without any intent to harm or be hurtful when they speak. Sometimes as children we would insult one another for the sake of being humorous. I recall during grade school how we would play the dozen or tell jokes about our parents, just for a laugh. That was obviously when I was a child. However, there is an obvious distinction between then and now. Paul elucidated the notable differences between childhood and adulthood from a spiritual perspective.

So now that we are in Christ, God does not want His children to continue playing the dozen with one another. On the contrary, He expects us to filter our words through love's strainer, and only allow words that are edifying and lovely to fall from our lips, being careful as we communicate with each other. Paul's short list is well chosen because as human beings mature, behavioral distinctions evolve during their walk with the Lord over the course of a lifetime. We don't expect a grown man to babble like a baby, nor do we expect a mature Christian to gossip, slander, or use profane and divisive language among the saints. We don't expect a woman to have fairy tale ideas about life the way she did as a little girl, nor should we expect a mature Christian woman to stir up division.

Admittedly, the final characteristic Paul used to hammer his point home; growth is required. Growth is extremely important to our overall maturation process. So much so, that when we fail to grow spiritually, we impede our ability to gain wisdom and use knowledge and understanding to our advantage. Ultimately, the hope we all have is there should come a time when we transition from our old way of thinking and living, leaving our worldly ways behind to become mature in our walk with the Lord. Paul emphasized his transition was evident once he became a mature believer.

Have you made this transition? Have you come to the realization that growth is required? Are you growing, or has your growth become stunted? Time to examine your own level of maturity and evaluate yourself against Jesus Christ; remain connected to the body of Christ and keep going. Live forward. Don't waste your pain.

Section III

Pain: Don't Waste It

Chapter 10

Don't Waste Your Pain

Pain. Suffering. Trials. Disappointments. Setbacks. However you refer to these unwelcome events, they are experiences we all face during one stage of life or another. As we have already cited, Jesus Christ expressly told his disciples, "*In the world you will have tribulation*" (John 16:33 ESV). Some translations read, "*In this world you will have trouble.*" (John 16:33 NIV) Regardless of the word used, the point is clear, no one will escape this life without facing some form of misfortune, distress, or woe.

Sometimes we tend to think or tell ourselves that we are the only one suffering when we are going through a personal ordeal. We act like no one has been through what we are experiencing, no one understands, and no one cares. However, nothing could be further from the truth. This is why the words of Jesus are so important to remember and store in our hearts. If Christ took the time to warn his disciples and they still suffered, why should we take suffering so personally?

One of the saddest ways we disturb ourselves is acting as if we have a monopoly on pain. This behavior is attributed to becoming self-obsessed, which generally starts as a result of an initial painful experience. If we fail to resolve the hurt and move forward day by day, we eventually keep dwelling on the event. This only sinks us into a deeper mode of depression and triggers feelings of isolation, rejection, and a cycle of ongoing self-examination, leading to self-effacement or dissing yourself. Sometimes we feel the need to devalue ourselves because we have allowed other people to define our worth.

Let me be supremely clear that no one can truly evaluate you because they did not give you value in the first place. We must realize only the creator of a thing can place value on that which was created. Once we agree with the words of the living God, which tell us we are *"fearfully and wonderfully made"* (Psalm 139:14 ESV), then we will stop seeking validation from others. Living in agreement with God is the start to working our way back and seeing ourselves as only God can. I realize this will take some adjustment because you have not spent much time thinking of yourself the way God does, but it is worth it in coming to grips with the fact that man cannot give you value nor rob you of your value.

The truth is, we are the only ones who can rob ourselves of our own value by behaving as if we need someone other than God to validate us. Do yourself a favor and never give anyone that type of power over you. And if you have made this a practice, stop it, and stop it now. This is the quickest way to form a codependent relationship whereby you always end up on the short end of the stick. Believe me when I say it is not too late to begin again, to start over and make a fresh start.   The fact that you are presently reading this book means you have a wonderful opportunity to use the painful experiences of your past to become a blessing to someone (or many people) on this journey called life. Maybe because of the broken feeling deep down inside your soul, you thought you were incapable of making a difference in anyone's life, let alone becoming a positive influence. But you are still breathing, my friend, and right now, today, you can pick yourself up and begin to become an encouragement to others. This is not despite what you have been through—no, but because you have suffered and survived the events and setbacks that you thought broke you.

You my friend can parlay yourself as a pearl that brightens someone's day because you recognized the jewel that was developed inside you through your pain. The illustration of the formation of pearls inside oysters is presented for you to appreciate that suffering does not have to break you; we must learn to accept that struggle produces endurance that could not be generated any other way. Your own struggle during and after painful experience produced a story only you have lived to tell, which has the potential to benefit others. The oyster's pearl can only come forth after the oyster suffers extreme irritation from a grain of sand trapped within. No grain of sand, no suffering; no suffering, no irritation; without the extreme and prolonged irritation—no pearl. Aren't you glad oysters can't tolerate sand?

As long as we don't allow our emotional health to decline, the irritants of life can serve as pearl generators for humanity's common good. The stories of how we survived and overcame mistakes we made can benefit others greatly when we abandon our self-centered ways to help someone else who has been knocked down.

Stop Looking for Validation: See Your God Given Worth

Another man cannot place value on that which God created. This is further proof that we must stop looking for fellow humans to validate us. Don't misunderstand me; I follow that most people seek out others to see if they are on track, on point, on fleek. However, this can become a dangerously addictive habit whereby we only seek out fellow humans to judge us and forget that God has already done a wonderful job when He designed us. What we need is someone to hold us accountable, not to assign us value. We need someone to show us our blind spots and tell us where we are missing the mark, not to evaluate and validate us.

The psalmist offers us the necessary adjustment to correct the mistake we make by seeking human acceptance. He provides the proper coordinates that help us avoid becoming lost in man's world of self-centered darkness. Do you see it? The first instruction he suggests, like a boss, is for us to look upward, stating, "I praise you..." I realize this is where our problem starts. We look around for someone other than God to praise us, for the gift God gave us, when in reality we possess gifts that only God can appraise.

The psalmist shuns the premise that someone other than God is worthy of giving praise, so they look to God and only God their creator for praise. In stanza 13 of this same psalm, God is credited for being the divine potter that masterfully molds and shapes them before they were born, known by the world, or seen by the human eye. The very place of our inception is the place where God first forms his human creation, masterfully handcrafting us with His own individual stamp of approval on each of our lives.

The psalmist clearly understands how important this individual stamp of approval is. He rushes to shout, "God, I praise you," because he has discerned that since God is responsible for crafting him, God alone is worthy of praise. Therefore, he looks up and he gives God praise. But not only does he give us an upward coordinate, but he also has us move from looking upward to looking inward, stating, *"for I am fearfully and wonderfully made"* (Psalm 139:14 ESV). This is the second step in helping us avoid the temptation of wrongfully subjecting ourselves to useless examination by other human beings.

Given that God is responsible for placing His stamp of approval on His creation, the only conclusion is: *we are fearfully and wonderfully made.* By using the word fearfully, the psalmist suggests we should recognize the need to express a certain awe of our own selves simply because God created us. This is not to suggest we become prideful and full of ourselves. The language of this stanza is meant to draw our attention toward the workmanship of the Creator, which makes us aware of the value and purpose we possess.

Because God created us, we should respect the imputed value He place in us, concluding, with a certain reverence, we are fearfully made. The perfect creator designed each of us with a perfect purpose. This should seal the deal for us that our value was imputed to us before we were born and is no less intact after we are born.

The psalmist helps assure us, one can give, take our lesson our value. Unfortunately, we are guilty of diminishing our own worth, purpose and value as we seek man to evaluate the worth God has bestowed upon us before we were born. Oh, how precious we are in the sight of God; wonderful are the works of His hands, and that indeed includes us. God instilled in us a purpose for living, and no matter how someone sees us, they cannot suppress, destroy, or devalue our purpose. However, we mistakenly do this all by ourselves, by being dissatisfied with God's copacetic critique of us: "fearfully and wonderfully made." Being created in God's image, we must learn to live with purpose and see our own worth. Rather than waiting for someone to bless us with their fallible evaluation of us. This makes us vulnerable for someone to throw shade our way, causing a cascading effect of emotional instability, leading to a sense of emotional dependance on the shade thrower.

Fearfully and Wonderfully Made: Your Creator Values You

How many of us would expect a renowned artist such as Picasso, to allow his buyers to set the price on his paintings, or a builder of a house to allow the buyers to set their own price on the purchase of a house for that matter? Strange how we would reject the notion of an artist or builder allowing someone to place a value on an object for sale, yet we allow mere mortals to place a value on our worth.

Please explain to me how we reject the idea that someone can place value on objects, but we don't have a problem with someone placing value on someone else's life. Ok, so you are acting as if you are not guilty of this wrongful behavior. Well, the truth is most of the people in the world have succumbed to this ridiculous behavior at least once. When we allow people to determine our value and worth by acting as if life is over because they have moved on from us; acting as if we need them to survive, or that they mean the world to us, and without them we are nothing—this is a clear indication that we have allowed someone to devalue our existence.

Oh, I realize you never gave much thought to the way you were behaving or how it gave someone the power to determine value on your life. Yet, this is the extent to which we grant mere mortals access to our true worth when we decide if we are valuable based on someone's acceptance or rejection of us in a relationship.

The verse resonates with that only the Creator can provide the correct assessment of man. *For the right to place value is only reserved for the one that created a thing, to give value to the thing they created. Therefore, since man had absolutely nothing, even remotely to do with the act of creation then we must work hard to reject subjecting ourselves to obscure observations that fail to accurately assess the creator's workmanship.* Nor should we feel devalued when another mortal oversteps their bounds and decides they are qualified to mishandle and mistreat God's creation.

This verse sets the record straight in so many ways: *I was wonderful when God created me, I was wonderful before I met you, and I will remain wonderful when you exit.* God alone gives us our value and God has already accepted that which He has created and concluded, "it is very good" (Genesis 1:31 ESV).

This is the turning point we all must make, accepting God's value of us as "fearfully and wonderfully made." Knowing this deep down inside and rejecting anything less than this is our own responsibility. See, when you learn to connect with the value God has placed within you, no one can make you feel like less. The truth is, God thought of us as such a valuable commodity in His creation that he sent His only Son to die for our sins. Now that proves we are truly more valuable than we ever realized. Therefore, never become guilty of devaluing yourself because someone does not see your true worth or walks away from you. This only means they were not a fit for you.

Live forward. Don't waste your pain.

Chapter 11

Conclusion

Know this, my friends: through the authority of scriptures and the grace afforded to us by the blood of the Lord Jesus Christ, we are not held hostage by the guilt and shame of our past mistakes, sins, faults, or failures (Romans 8:1-3; 2 Corinthians 5:17; Psalm 103:12). Therefore, if the God of the universe is not condemning those who have accepted grace through faith, do yourself a favor and stop throwing a gloomy cloud over your life. Cut yourself some slack. Don't count your mistakes and worry about time behind you or the time in front of you. Live forward!

I have always been an avid fan of organized sports. Two of my favorite sports have in common that the games are played in two halves—four quarters. Additionally, both sports allow for overtime when a game's regulation time concludes with a tied score. Over the years, I have witnessed some amazing games with unbelievable comebacks. After being counted out and so far behind in points throughout the game, basketball and football teams can rally and win incredible shakeup victories, thrilling for a sports fan like myself. Many times, fans begin to walk out when they believe a win is beyond reach. They count their team out, figure the game is over even before regulation time runs out.

The simple truth is, the best game rebounds and turnovers are only possible when there is still time left on the clock and the underdog team keeps fighting to win. The losing team becomes the champion team because despite insurmountable odds, they keep working every strategy to beat the competition and win. Are you with me?

Although fans don't always believe, the players, the people who matter most, must never count themselves out or stop trying. The first time I understood the confidence required of players regardless of the score, was at the end of a third quarter, when I saw players holding up four fingers. At first, I didn't understand this gesture, until I realized the four fingers are symbolic of the fourth quarter starting. In that moment of any and every game, the first three quarters hardly matter, the score does not matter, performance during the earlier quarters doesn't matter. All that matters is the fourth quarter, the time left on the clock and what they do with it. The players understand the game is played in two halves and four quarters, and they must have confidence to believe that if they keep fighting, just keep going, they can own the fourth quarter, finish strong, and pull out a victory. This kind of heart, spirit, and will to win is what creates champion legacies.

My friends, you may find yourself in the fourth quarter of your life. Maybe the first three have not turned out all that great for you. You may have fumbled some opportunities or made mistakes that set you back. Maybe you feel too far behind to meet your goals. Maybe it seems too hard to hold your confidence and win in life. May I suggest you adjust your perspective and boost your attitude. Consider that you are still here, you still have time left in the game of life. YOU CAN STILL WIN.

The story of Samson presents a view of life in halves and quarters. In the first quarter of his life, he killed a lion, revealing his special gift and signaling a divine assignment placed be. The second quarter of his life he lost a wife and avenged her death by killing those responsible. In the third quarter of his life, he chose to play tricks in the red zone and flirt with a vixen, only to lose his strength, his eyesight, his dignity, and his freedom.

For all intents and purposes Samson lost the game of life, failed himself, and failed his God, but he never gave up on God and God never gave up on Samson. Samson utilized the one winning strategy that is at all our disposal, he turned back to God. If you still desire to win, turn to God. Forget the first half of your life, forget your earlier performance, and turn to God and win. Why should you turn to God? Simple, read the word of the Lord; *"For I know the plans I have for you, declares the LORD, plans for welfare and not for evil, to give you a future and a hope"* (Jeremiah 29:11 ESV).

Look at the above statement this way: God holds the playbook for each of our lives. Each one of us has a special playbook. Each player's responsibility is to arrive on time and learn the plays before taking the field. The players that achieve the most success are the ones who are familiar with the playbook and know exactly what their assignment is for each play.

The same is true with us. God owns the playbook, and we are simply players on his team. Our job is to seek God through His word, study and learn the playbook, and live life according to the bible. As it is written in Jerimiah: if we seek God and His plan for our lives, we will discover welfare, hope, and a bright future.

Hold up your head and four fingers. Look at your life in two halves and then four quarters. Perhaps your fourth quarter has just started. Use the strategies that will propel you toward success; keep fighting, keep working, turn your life over to God, and win.

After all of this, if you are still feeling a little despondent, just know that God controls the clock. God establishes the rules of the game and God does allow overtime! Live forward!

Citations

[i] Art Mathias, In His Image, (Anchorage: Wellspring Publishing, 2003), 37
[ii] Mathias, In His Image, 37
[iii] Maurice Watson, Looking Up When Life's Got You Down, (Atlanta: Dream Releaser Publishing, 2010), 18, 19
[iv] Dr. Maurice Watson, Looking Up When Life's Got You Down (Atlanta: Dream Releaser Publishing, 2010), 32
[v] R. T. Kendall, God Meant It for Good, (Wilkesboro: Morningstar Publications,2003), 122
[vi] Max Lucado, Facing Your Giants, (Nashville: Thomas Nelson Publisher, 2006), 69
[viivii] Byrd Baggett, Dare to Soar, (Successories, Inc, 1997), 37
[viii] Max Lucado, Facing Your Giants, 94
[ixix] Ray Pritchard, An Anchor for the Soul, (Chicago: Moody Publishers, 2000), 129
[x] Don Moen, Give Thanks (2015)
[xi] GWMA Youth Mass Choir, (May 2010)
[xii] Walter Hawkins, Be Grateful (1978)
[xiii] Joyce Meyer, Me and My Big Mouth, (Oklahoma: Harrison House, Inc., 1997), 99, 100

About the Author:

W. C. Wilson is a graduate of Florida A & M University. He is currently an active member of the Shiloh Metropolitan Missionary Baptist Church in Jacksonville, Florida. He serves as one of the Elders, one of the Bible Study Fellowship teachers, a member of the Prison Ministry, as well as on the Partners in Prayer Team.

The author attended Trinity Theological Seminary, earning the degree of Master of Arts in Pastoral Ministry, and receiving training in Nouthetic Counseling.

The author has a passion for seeing God's children become fully grown, mature, not lacking anything. Therefore, as stated by the apostle Paul, "Forgetting what lies behind and straining forward to what lies ahead", Philippians 3:13b ESV; he encourages them to, "Live life Forward".